"What ha

"Will happe⋯⋯⋯⋯⋯⋯⋯⋯⋯⋯⋯ce we set is up to you, but the end result is inevitable."

Zara shifted to face him. "I need this job."

"I assumed so, that's why I hired you." *Well, one of the reasons.* "And the job has nothing to do with what's going on between us."

"Nothing is going on," she all but yelled. "Nothing can go on. Not while I'm working for you."

"Fine. You're fired."

Zara glared at him. "That's ridiculous."

"I always get what I want, Zara."

"And you're that desperate for a bedmate?"

Leaning forward, his fingertips found the side of her face, stroking down to her neck where she trembled. "No. Just you."

"Why?" she whispered.

"Why not?" he retorted.

His hand came up to cup the side of her face. He stroked her lip as his other hand cupped the back of her head. A soft sigh escaped her.

"You're not thinking work right now, are you? You're concentrating on my touch, on how you want more."

"What are you doing to me?"

"Proving a point."

* * *

Trapped with the Tycoon is part of the Mafia Moguls series: For this tight-knit mob family, going legitimate leads to love!

Dear Reader,

Okay, who doesn't love a bad boy? Let's just be honest here, shall we? Bad boys are hot, they're sexy and they make us all giddy to see rules broken.

I'm so excited to introduce you all to my bad boys of Boston! In this first book of my Mafia Moguls series, you'll meet the O'Sheas. Two brothers, a sister and one black sheep who is like family to this Irish clan.

It's going to take a special woman to tame Braden O'Shea, especially since he just took over as head of the family business. He has an agenda to get back what belongs to his family and if he has to use his latest associate, then so be it. Zara is a strong woman and nothing scares her...except her feelings for this bad boy. It's her strength and determination that have Braden falling fast and hard.

Oh, and I had to throw in a blizzard because, well...it's fun! Not to me, but in a fictitious world. :)

I hope you enjoy Braden and Zara and the O'Shea family saga. There's nothing better than secrets, lies, betrayal... all the juicy things we come to love in our stories.

So sit back, relax and enjoy this whirlwind love affair!

Jules Bennet

TRAPPED WITH THE TYCOON

JULES BENNETT

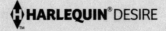

HARLEQUIN®DESIRE

Recycling programs
for this product may
not exist in your area.

ISBN-13: 978-0-373-73437-5

Trapped with the Tycoon

Copyright © 2016 by Jules Bennett

This edition published by arrangement with Harlequin Books S.A.

For questions and comments about the quality of this book,
please contact us at CustomerService@Harlequin.com.

® and TM are trademarks of Harlequin Enterprises Limited or its
corporate affiliates. Trademarks indicated with ® are registered in the
United States Patent and Trademark Office, the Canadian Intellectual
Property Office and in other countries.

Printed in U.S.A.

Award-winning author **Jules Bennett** is no stranger to romance—she met her husband when she was only fourteen. After dating through high school, the two married. He encouraged her to chase her dream of becoming an author. Jules has now published nearly thirty novels. She and her husband are living their own happily-ever-after while raising two girls. Jules loves to hear from readers through her website, julesbennett.com, her Facebook fan page or on Twitter.

Books by Jules Bennett

Harlequin Desire

What the Prince Wants
A Royal Amnesia Scandal
Maid for a Magnate

The Barrington Trilogy

When Opposites Attract...
Single Man Meets Single Mom
Carrying the Lost Heir's Child

Mafia Moguls

Trapped with the Tycoon

Harlequin Special Edition

The St. Johns of Stonerock

Dr. Daddy's Perfect Christmas
The Fireman's Ready-Made Family
From Best Friend to Bride

Visit the Author Profile page
at Harlequin.com, or
julesbennett.com, for more titles.

When I proposed a mafia series for
Harlequin Desire, I had no idea how it
would go over with my editor. But when
Stacy Boyd's face lit up with excitement,
I knew we were on the same page...literally.
This book is for you, Stacy!

One

The second her ex's fingers closed around her arm, Zara Perkins jerked from the firm grasp. "I'm not dancing, I'm working."

Having Shane Chapman show up at the biggest job she'd ever taken on for the most prestigious family she'd ever worked for was just her luck. She prided herself on her business, on doing everything in her power to make her clients' parties the event they hired her for. And Shane could ruin it all.

"You're such a tease," he mocked, the whiskey on his breath repugnant. "I saw you looking at me."

Sure, with disdain when she realized he was in attendance. She'd rather walk barefoot over shards of glass than let his arms wrap around her. Zara prayed Shane would go away. This was a new job, a job she desperately needed. The last thing she wanted to do was have to defend a man she had the misfortune of dating a few times.

"Dance with me."

The low, demanding words sent shivers through her body. Zara knew without turning around who would be behind her…her new employer and rumored-to-be corrupt business mogul Braden O'Shea.

With Shane directly in front of her and Braden behind her, Zara was literally stuck in the exact predicament she didn't want to be in on her first big night of working for the O'Sheas. But right now, she was bracketed by two powerful men. One she wanted nothing to do with and the other set her heart racing as only a mysterious, intriguing man could do. The few times she'd been in his office had been a bit difficult to concentrate. Braden O'Shea exuded authority, control and sex appeal.

Humiliation flooded her at the idea that Braden had to intervene. She was here in a professional capacity. Having her ex confront her was not exactly showcasing the reputation she'd worked so hard to build, and coming off as anything less than professional could be career suicide.

Shane glared over her shoulder, silently telling Braden precisely what he thought of the interruption, but before Zara could say a word to either man, Braden took hold of her arm and pulled her to the dance area in the ballroom of his lavish, historical home.

Instantly she was plastered against the oldest of the O'Shea siblings…not a difficult position to find herself in, actually. She had often appreciated the visual of his broad, sexy body wrapped in the finest of black suits with black shirt and no tie. But being up close and personal, breathing in what was undoubtedly expensive, masculine cologne that had her eyes fluttering closed as she inhaled, was another level of torture entirely.

The man exuded sex appeal, but he was her new boss, and she needed this job for the prestige and the insanely large paycheck. This was her first official event with this prominent family after being officially hired a few months ago. Screwups…screwing of *any* kind…was not allowed.

So, no sex thoughts. None. Okay, maybe later when she was alone.

"I really need to be working."

A little protest was in order, wasn't it? Even if sliding against Braden felt like some sort of foreplay in itself, she was the events coordinator for this party. Dancing with the host and boss was a major professional no-no, even if they'd always gotten along well with each other before tonight. There'd always been some ridiculous magnetic energy between them that she'd never experienced before but refused to explore.

Braden's dark gaze studied her, his mouth unsmiling. "With a dress like that, you should be dancing."

The sexual undertone wasn't lost on her. She'd thrown on her go-to black dress with a low V in the back and front, long sleeves, with the hem stopping at her knees. The dress was simple, yet made a statement. Hiding her curves wasn't an option unless she wore a muumuu. Besides, this was the best dress she'd found in her boxes of belongings since she hadn't unpacked from her move…three months ago. Because unpacking meant settling in, making roots.

"You're not paying me to dance," she told him, though she made no motion to step out of his powerful embrace. Her mind told her this wasn't professional, but her stubborn body wasn't getting that memo. "I'm positive this isn't professional to ignore my position here."

"You're on break."

With one large hand at the small of her back and the other gripping hers, Braden led her in a dance to an old classic. Crystal chandeliers suspended from the ceiling, illuminating the polished wood floor in a kaleidoscope of colors. The wall of French doors leading to the patio gave the room an even larger feel. The O'Sheas were known for their lavish parties, and now that she was in the ballroom, she could see why. Who had an actual ballroom in their house?

Other couples swirled around them, but with few words

and those dark, mesmerizing eyes, this man captured her undivided attention. She needed to get back control over this situation because even though Braden insisted she was taking a break, she wasn't paid to socialize. She was given an insane amount of money to make this annual party an even bigger success than the last one, and she'd heard a rumor the last events coordinator for the O'Sheas was fired in the most humiliating of circumstances. She couldn't afford slipups.

Or crazy exes.

"I could've handled him," she told Braden. "Shane was just…"

"I'm not talking about another man when I have a beautiful woman in my arms."

Okay, yeah, that definitely crossed the professional threshold. Each word he spoke dripped with charm, authority… desire. He held his feelings back, remained in control at all times. From what she'd seen, he was calculating, powerful and the aura of mystery surrounding him was even more alluring and sexy.

But, no. She'd just ended things with one powerful, controlling man. She was fine being single and focusing on her year-old business. Her goal was to be the company all major names turned to when needing a party planned or hosting a special event. Having the O'Sheas was a huge leap in the right direction. No matter the rumors surrounding their, well, less-than-legal operations behind the front of their world-renowned auction house, the O'Sheas had connections she could only dream of. She hoped this event led to new clients.

"If you keep scowling, I'm going to think you prefer Shane's company," Braden stated, breaking into her thoughts. "Or maybe I interrupted a lover's quarrel?"

Zara nearly recoiled. "No. Definitely not a lover's quarrel."

Had Braden overheard what Shane had said? Heat flooded her cheeks. She'd dated Shane briefly and had broken things off with him weeks ago, yet the man was relentless in trying to get her attention again. When they'd gone on only a few dates, he'd started getting a bit too controlling for her comfort. Thankfully she hadn't slept with him.

Still, he'd made a point to tell her how fast he could ruin her business. Did he honestly think that would make her give him another chance? Threats were *so* not the way to a woman's heart.

She wasn't one to back down without a fight, but she was realistic, and Shane did have money and connections. She shivered at the severity of his words.

"Cold?" Braden asked.

Braden's hand drifted up, his fingertips grazed across her bare skin just above the dip in her material.

With the heat in his eyes, there was no way she could claim a chill. The firmness of his body moved perfectly with hers; that friction alone could cause a woman to go up in flames.

"Mr. O'Shea—"

"Braden."

Zara swallowed. "Fine. Braden," she corrected, forcing herself to hold his heavy-lidded stare. "I really should check on the drinks—"

"Taken care of."

"The hors d'oeuvres—"

"Are fine."

He spun her toward the edge of the dance floor, closer to one set of French doors leading out on to the patio. Snow swirled around outside; a storm for later tonight was in the forecast. February in Boston could be treacherous and unpredictable.

"You've done a remarkable job with this evening," he told her. "I'm impressed."

She couldn't suppress the smile. "I'm relieved to hear that. I love my job and want all of my clients happy. Still, dancing when I should be working isn't something I make a habit of."

His thumb continued to lightly stroke the bare skin on her back. The man was potent, sparking arousal without even trying. Or maybe he *was* trying and he was so stellar at being charming, she couldn't tell.

It took her a moment to realize that Braden had maneuvered her into a corner. With his back to the dancers, he shielded her completely with those broad shoulders and pinned her with that dark, mesmerizing gaze. "I heard what he said to you."

Zara froze, took a deep breath and chose her next words carefully. "I assure you I would never let anyone or anything affect my ability to work. Shane is—"

"Not going to bother you again," he assured her with a promising yet menacing tone. Braden's eyes darted over her body, touching her just the same as his talented fingertips had done mere moments ago.

No. No, no, no. Hadn't she already scolded herself for having lustful thoughts? He was her boss, for pity's sake. No matter how intriguing Braden O'Shea was, she had no room for sex in her life right now. No wonder she was grouchy.

"Storm is kicking up." Braden nodded over her shoulder toward the floor-to-ceiling window. "Do you live far?"

"Maybe twenty minutes away."

"If you need to leave—"

"No." Zara shook her head, holding a hand up to stop him. "I've lived in Boston my entire life. Snow doesn't bother me. Besides, I would never leave an event early."

Braden studied her a moment before nodding. "I'm happy to hear that, but I don't want you driving on these roads. My driver will make sure you get home."

"There's no need for that."

Braden leaned in, just enough for her to feel his breath on her cheek. "Let's not waste time arguing when we should be dancing."

Snaking an arm around her waist, he pulled her against his body once again. Apparently her break wasn't over. Good thing, because she wasn't quite ready to leave the luxury of brushing against his taut body.

Her curves were killer from a visual standpoint, but to have them beneath his hands was damn near crippling. Braden knew she was a sexy woman, but he hadn't expected this sizzling attraction. He had a plan and he needed to stay focused. Those damn curves momentarily threw him off his game.

Zara in her elegant black cocktail dress with a plunging neckline showcasing the swell of her breasts was absolutely stunning, eye-catching and causing him to lose focus on the true intent of this party.

Which was why he hadn't missed the encounter when one of his most hated enemies sidled up next to the woman Braden had been gazing at off and on earlier in the evening. A flash of jealousy had speared him. Ridiculous, since Zara was merely the events coordinator…and that job had not come about by chance. Braden had purposely chosen her. He needed to get closer, close enough to gain access into her personal, private life and into her home. His family's heritage could be hidden in her house, and she'd have no clue if she stumbled upon the items.

Nothing could keep him from fulfilling his deathbed promise to his dad.

Braden was all for adding in a little seduction on his way to gaining everything he'd ever wanted. Pillow talk always loosened the tongue, and if Zara could tell him everything he needed to know, then he wouldn't have to break any laws…at least where she was concerned. He'd be a fool to turn that combination down and there was no way he could ignore how her body moved so perfectly against his. He also hadn't missed how her breath had caught the second he'd touched her exposed back. He had to admit, just to himself, the innocent touch had twisted something in him, as well. Arousal was a strong, overwhelming emotion, and one he had to keep control over.

For now, he needed to remember he was the head of the family and as the leader, he had a duty to fulfill. Flirting, seducing and even a little extracurricular activities were fine, so long as he kept his eye on the target.

Tonight O'Shea's Auction House was celebrating not only being a prominent, world-renowned auction house for over eighty years, but also the opening of two more satellite locations in Atlanta and Miami, thanks to his brother, Mac, who had moved down to Miami to oversee the properties.

Boston would always be home to the main store, Braden's store, now that his father was gone. And now that Braden was fully in charge, there were going to be some changes. This family had to move toward being legit. The stress and pressure Braden had seen his father go through wasn't something Braden wanted for his future. The massive heart attack that stole Patrick O'Shea's life wasn't brought on by leading a normal, worry-free life.

Braden had a five-year plan. Surely in that time they could remove themselves from any illegal ties and slowly sever those bonds. The killings had to stop. That was the first order of business, but tonight, after seeing Shane manhandle Zara, Braden was almost ready to go back on his vow.

Death was nothing new to him. He'd witnessed his father give a kill order multiple times for reasons he'd always justified. Braden may not have always agreed with his father's ways, but his father was an effective businessman and well respected.

Zara's deep chocolate eyes shifted around the room before landing back on him. "Your brother is coming this way."

Braden didn't turn, didn't relinquish his hold on Zara.

The music continued, guests around them danced and chatted, but Braden paid them no mind.

"We need to talk," Mac stated.

Braden stopped dancing but didn't let go of Zara as he threw Mac a glance over his shoulder. "I'll meet you in the study in five minutes."

"Now."

Braden resisted the urge to curse. He prided himself on control. "Five minutes," he said, before turning back and focusing solely on Zara.

He picked up right where they'd left off dancing. He could still feel Mac behind him, so Braden maneuvered his partner toward the edge of the dance floor. Zara was his for now, and sharing their time wasn't an option.

"You can go talk to him." Zara smiled, a deep dimple winking back at him. The innocence of the dimple and the sex appeal of that dress were polar opposite. "I should be working anyway, you know."

He *was* paying her to work, but that didn't mean he didn't like the feel of her in his arms, against him. There would be time for more later. He'd make sure of it. Gaining her trust on a personal level would lead him exactly where he needed to be.

Gliding his fingertips over her exposed back one last time, Braden stepped away from Zara and tipped his head. "I'll find you when I'm done with Mac. If you have any more problems with Shane, you come straight to me."

Zara nodded, clasping her hands in front of her and searching the room as if trying to get a location on the man in question. "I'll be fine. Go talk to your brother, and thank you for the dance. I have to get back to work."

Braden closed the space between them, picked up her hand and kissed her delicate knuckles. "I should be thanking you."

Her mouth parted as she let out a slight gasp when his lips grazed her hand. Yes, enticing her would be no problem at all. He'd been waiting on the right opportunity, the moment he could get the greatest impact out of this game of seduction.

First things first, he had to see what the issue was with his younger brother. Braden excused himself and went in search of Mac.

The entire O'Shea family had come for the party despite the bad weather predictions for the Boston area, including cousins from Boston and down the East Coast, his brother, sister and Ryker.

What kind of celebration would this be for the O'Sheas if the whole Irish clan didn't attend? Mac would be overseeing the southern locations, a job he was all too eager to take over and to get out of the cold winters for, especially since his best friend, Jenna, had moved to Miami about a year ago.

Once in the study, Braden closed the door behind him and crossed the polished wood floors. Mac leaned against the old mahogany desk, swirling bourbon around in his tumbler. Braden knew it was bourbon without even asking because the O'Sheas were simple men with simple needs—power, good bourbon and women. The order varied depending on the circumstance.

"You need to calm down," Mac commanded. "That murderous look in your eyes is scaring our guests."

"I'm calm." To prove it, Braden flashed a smile. "See?"

Mac shook his head. "Listen, I know you hate Shane Chapman. We all do. He's a lying prick. But, whatever his personal—"

"He's harassing Zara."

Braden stopped short just before he reached his brother and crossed his arms over his chest. Shane Chapman was the bane of the O'Sheas' existence. A few years ago, he'd attempted to hire the auction house to acquire an heirloom illegally. Braden had made a valiant effort to get it, spending more time and money than he really should've, but to no avail.

Viewing it as a deliberate slight, Shane had attempted to blackmail the O'Sheas. His laughable threats were quickly taken care of by means nobody discussed. Shane was lucky he was still breathing because that had been during the Patrick O'Shea reign.

Shane was only at this party for one reason—the whole "keep your friends close and your enemies closer" wasn't just a clever saying.

"Keep your eye on him," Braden went on. "This can't interfere with the plans. If Shane needs to go…"

Mac nodded. "I'll let Ryker know."

Ryker. The O'Sheas' right-hand man, who may as well have been born into the family. Instead, he'd been unofficially adopted as a rebellious preteen, and he'd been with them since.

But damn it, Braden didn't want blood on his hands. He wanted to concentrate on retrieving the heirlooms and relics their auction house was officially known for. They had an elite list of clients, and word of mouth always brought more on board. The timeless pieces the O'Sheas uncovered all over the world kept their business thriving. Several pieces were "discovered" by less-than-legal means, but they were paid hefty sums to be discreet. Smuggling in items with legal loads for big auctions was easy to do.

"I think your approach to Zara isn't the smartest." Mac sipped his bourbon. "You're coming on too strong and not focusing."

Braden narrowed his gaze. "That's a pretty bold statement coming from the man who has a woman in every major city."

Mac eyed him over the glass. "We're not talking about me. Unless you'd like me to seduce the beautiful party planner."

"Keep your damn hands off her."

Why was he suddenly so territorial? Braden had no claims on Zara.

But he'd held her, felt her against him and seen a thread of vulnerability when Zara had been looking at Shane. He refused to see any woman harassed or mistreated.

His sister, Laney, was currently dating some schmuck, who could be demeaning at times. Yet another issue Braden would deal with now that he was in charge. No way in hell would he allow his baby sister to be belittled by anyone. Ever.

"Leave Zara to me, and you concentrate on your new locations," Braden told his brother. "Is that all you needed?"

Mac finished off his drink, setting his tumbler down on the desk. "For now. I'll keep an eye on Shane. Ryker will be a last resort. I know you want to move in a different direction, but Shane can't interfere. We're too close to finding those scrolls."

Braden nodded and headed back out to the party. Those scrolls, all nine of them, were centuries old and held immense power over Braden's family. He wanted them back, and at one time, during the Great Depression, they'd been in the home Zara currently lived in. Supposedly they'd been stored in a trunk that had been sold decades ago. Unfortunately, the trunk had been recently tracked down but as the scrolls hadn't been inside, they were back to square one with Zara's house as the last known location.

Just as Braden cleared the wide opening leading to the ballroom, he spotted Shane standing over Zara. She shook her head and started to turn when Shane's hand whipped out and gripped her bicep, jerking her back to his chest.

Braden didn't care about moving stealthily through the crowd. He felt Mac right behind him as he charged forward. His brother always had his back.

"Remove your hand from Miss Perkins's arm." Braden didn't try to mask the rage in his tone. He waited a beat, but Shane still held tight and kept his back to Braden. "Remove your hand or I won't need to get my security team. I'll throw your ass out myself."

Over his shoulder, Braden heard Mac telling someone, most likely one of their employees, to have security on standby. Braden knew Mac was only looking out for everyone's best interest, but Braden could only see red right now. Thankfully, Shane had backed Zara into a corner, and the guests were still milling about, oblivious to the action.

Shane threw a glance over his shoulder. "This doesn't concern you. Zara and I have a little unfinished business. Just a lover's spat."

The look on her face told Braden there wasn't anything unfinished here and this sure as hell wasn't a lover's spat—she'd told him as much earlier.

Zara's wide, dark eyes held his. Even though she had her chin tipped up in defiance, her lips thinned in anger, there was a spark of fear in those eyes, and Braden wouldn't tolerate Shane one more second.

Braden grabbed on to Shane's wrist, applying pressure in the exact spot to cause maximum pain. "Take your damn hand off her. Now."

Shane gave Zara's arm a shove. "You can't keep avoiding me," he told her, rubbing his wrist where Braden had squeezed. "Next time I call, you better answer or I'll come by your office. I doubt you want that."

Just as Shane turned, Braden blocked his exit. "If you ever touch her or any woman that way again and I hear of it, you'll wish for death. Feel me?"

Shane hesitated a second before he laughed, slapping Braden on the shoulder. "You're Patrick O'Shea's son, right down to the threats. And here I thought you were too good to get your hands dirty."

Even though the bastard had touched Braden, he wasn't about to take the bait Shane dangled in front of him. Flexing his fists, Braden was more than ready to hit Shane, but he knew deep down he wasn't like his father.

Braden had never ordered anyone to be killed, had always said he wouldn't. Right now, though, he was reconsidering that promise he'd made to himself.

"There's a first time for everything," he promised just as two security men in black suits came to show Shane the door.

They didn't put their hands on him, as that would've caused even more of a scene, but they did flank either side of the nuisance and walk him toward the closest exit. People around him stared for only a moment before going back to their conversations. Nearly everyone knew to mind their business if they wanted to remain in the O'Sheas' tight circle.

As soon as Shane was gone, Braden went back in with Zara.

"You okay here?" Mac whispered behind him.

With a nod, Braden wrapped his arm around Zara's waist. "We're fine. Cover for me." He silently led her to the small sitting room off the ballroom and closed the door behind him before turning to face Zara. She rubbed her arm, and it took all of Braden's willpower not to rush back out and follow through on his need to punch Shane.

Braden gently took Zara's other arm, trying to ignore the brush of his knuckles against the side of her breast, and guided her toward one of the leather club chairs.

Flicking on the light on the accent table by the chair, Braden squatted down in front of her.

"Braden—"

He held up his hand, cutting her off. "Let me see your arm."

"I'm fine. I really need to get back to work. I'm sorry I caused a scene."

"Either pull your sleeve up or pull the shoulder down so I can see."

Zara hesitated a moment, then pulled the material off her shoulder, exposing creamy white skin and a royal blue strap from her bra. She shrugged enough to pull her arm up a bit.

Rage bubbled within Braden at the sight of blue finger-print-shaped bruises already forming on her flawless skin. "I should've knocked him out."

Slowly, Braden eased the material back over her arm and shoulder. Her eyes held his and her body trembled as she placed her hand over his, halting his movement.

"I'm fine," she assured him again. "I really need to get back to work. I appreciate what you did, though."

He hadn't realized how close he'd gotten until he felt her soft breath on his cheek. He glanced up to her, his eyes darting down to her lips.

"My motives aren't always so selfless."

The corner of her mouth quirked. "Whatever your motives are, they were effective."

He leaned in closer, close enough that barely a breath could pass between their lips. "I'm always effective."

Two

Effective. Thorough. Protective. So many adjectives could be used to describe Braden O'Shea. Yet he'd come to her defense without question earlier when Shane had snapped.

Zara nestled deeper into her coat as the heat from Braden's SUV hit her. This dress had been such a good idea when she'd been inside. Now that the snow was near blizzard-like conditions, not so much. She'd had to swap her sexy heels for snow boots, which she'd packed with her once she'd seen the forecast. So now the allure of her favorite LBD was lost thanks to the thick, rubber-soled, sensible shoes.

"When you said you'd have your driver bring me home, I didn't know you were the driver." She glanced over, taking in his profile illuminated from the glowing dash lights. In the dark, Braden seemed even more mysterious, more enigmatic.

"After the incident with Shane, I'm not placing your safety in anyone else's hands." He gripped the wheel as the tires slid, then gained traction again. "I wouldn't want you driving in this mess anyway. I heard a couple at the party say the forecasters mentioned feet instead of inches."

Zara's breath caught in her throat as Braden carefully maneuvered around a slick corner with skill. The back end fishtailed before he righted the vehicle. They'd only passed two other cars since leaving his historic Beacon Hill mansion.

"I'm so sorry about this," she told him, once the car was on a straight path and she could focus on breathing normally. "I should've left when you suggested it earlier because of the bad weather. Then Shane wouldn't have been a problem, and you wouldn't be out in this mess."

"Shane will be a problem until he meets his match." Braden flashed her a wicked grin that looked even more ominous due to the minimal lighting. There was also the veiled implication that Braden was the perfect match for Shane. "As for the weather, don't worry about it. This storm came on faster than I thought, and I have nothing else to do tonight."

"Hopefully the guests all made it home okay," she said, voicing her thoughts. The caterers had left around the same time she did, so hopefully they were safe, too. "They left over an hour ago, so maybe it wasn't too bad then."

She'd stayed behind to clean up and make sure the place was just as it had been before she'd entered—as she did with every event. All part of the party-planning business. Still, there would be a few people left from the cleaning service. She hoped they all got home okay, as well.

"You live alone?"

Braden's question sliced through the quiet. As if she could actually forget she was this close to the world's sexiest man. Then again, she didn't know every man in the world, but she'd still put Braden O'Shea and his sultry eyes and broad frame against anyone.

"Yes. I actually just moved into my grandmother's home three months ago. She'd just passed away, and I'm the only relative she had left."

"Sorry about your loss." In a move that surprised her, Braden reached across the console and squeezed her hand in a gesture of comfort before easing back. She didn't take him for the comforting type, but she knew in her heart his words and his touch were sincere.

"My father has been gone six months," he went on, his tone understanding. "On one hand, it seems like yesterday. On the other, I feel like I'm going to wake up from a nightmare and he'll be fine. None of us had a clue his heart was so bad."

Zara swallowed. She knew that nightmare-versus-reality feeling all too well. In the midst of her fantasizing over Braden, she'd not figured in the fact this man was still vulnerable, still suffering from a loss just as big as her own. Great, she'd not only been unprofessional tonight, she'd also been heartless.

"It's rough." For the first time since her grandmother's passing, Zara felt comfortable opening up to someone. Shane certainly hadn't been consoling in the few times they'd dated...another red flag where he'd been concerned. "Living in her home feels strange. I remember sleeping over there when I was little, but now it just seems so much larger, so empty."

Zara had never been afraid to live alone, but in a house this size, she was a little creeped out at night—the old ghost rumors didn't help, either. Perhaps once she rid the house of some of the antiques and actually unpacked her own things, that would help the place feel more like home. But she wasn't to that point yet. Removing her grandmother's favorite things just didn't seem right yet. And unpacking... Definitely not something Zara was comfortable with. A shrink would have a blast digging inside her mind over the reasons Zara had a fear of commitment even when it came to a house.

Red-and-blue flashing lights lit up behind them. Braden threw a glance in the mirror, his jaw clenched as he maneuvered cautiously to the side of the road.

Zara tensed, gripping her coat even tighter. What was wrong? They certainly hadn't been speeding. The rumors about the O'Sheas having illegal operations going flooded her mind. She didn't know whether the myth was true or false and it wasn't her place to judge, but she couldn't help but wonder. All she knew was they were powerful and they were paying her well. Oh, and Braden was the sexiest man she'd ever laid eyes, or hands, on.

Braden glanced at her. "Don't say anything."

Stunned, Zara nodded. What would she say?

Braden put his window down as the officer approached. "Evening, Officer."

The trooper leaned down and looked into the car. "The roads are at a level two now, and they're getting ready to up that to a three. Are you folks out because of an emergency?"

"No, sir. I'm giving my employee a ride home because I didn't think it was safe for her to be out alone."

The officer's eyes scanned over Zara, and she offered a slight smile.

"How far away is her house?"

"Just right up the street," Braden said, pointing. Zara had given him directions before they'd started out, and they were actually only a few houses away from hers.

"I suggest you plan on staying put once you drop her off. Any drivers caught out once the level three goes into effect will be ticketed," the officer stated. "I'll follow you to make sure you get there all right."

The full impact of the trooper's words hit Zara fast. Braden had to stay put? As in…stay the night? At her house? A ball of nerves quickly formed in her stomach. Her boss was spending the night? Her boss, whom she found utterly sexy and nearly irresistible, and there was already crackling sexual tension charging between them? Sure, this would be no problem at all.

"Thank you, Officer," Braden replied "We appreciate that."

Braden rolled his window up as the officer went back to his car. Silence filled the vehicle, and the weight of what was about to happen settled between them.

Zara risked a glance at Braden, but he didn't seem affected one bit. He kept his eyes forward, occasionally checking his mirrors as he pulled right into her drive. The cop gave a honk as he passed on by. Braden maneuvered the SUV around the slight curve that led to the detached garage around back.

Once he parked and killed the engine, Zara couldn't take the tension another second. She unfastened and turned to face him.

"I'm so sorry," she started. "Had I known you'd have to stay, I wouldn't have let you bring me home."

Braden threw her a lopsided smile. "No reason to be sorry. I don't mind spending the night with a beautiful woman."

Braden was well aware of his power. Hell, everyone who'd ever heard the name O'Shea knew the authority this family possessed. They even had a few of the local cops and federal agents in their back pockets…which had kept them out of the proverbial hot water more than once.

But even Braden couldn't have planned the timing of this snowstorm better, or the condition of the roads. Under different circumstances, he probably would've chanced driving back home regardless of the officer's warning. Wouldn't be the first time he'd gone against the law. But why would he want to leave? A forced stay at Zara's home was the green light he'd been waiting for, and it had come so much sooner than he'd ever intended. No way in hell was he leaving now. Not when this sexual chemistry between them had skyrocketed since he'd held her in his arms.

As he pulled his vehicle up to the garage, the streetlights went out. He cursed under his breath as the entire street was plunged into black. "Looks like the power went."

"Great," Zara muttered. "I don't have a generator. But I do have some heat that isn't electric. I've only used those gas logs once in my bedroom, and I've never tried to light the ones in the living room. Guess I'll have to figure it out in the dark."

Braden didn't know what got his blood pumping more: the fact he'd be able to fulfill his father's dying request and search this house, or the fact he'd be all alone in the dark with his sexy new employee.

He pulled to a stop by her back door. "Stay there. I'll come around to help you in."

He didn't wait for her to agree as he hopped out into the freezing temps to round the hood, using his phone to light a path. Even though he was still wearing his suit from the party, he'd thought ahead and changed from his dress shoes to his boots.

Jerking on the frozen handle, Braden opened the passenger door and took Zara's gloved hand as he settled his arm around her waist. The second she slid down from her seat, her body fell flush against his—well, as flush as it could be with the layers between them. Zara tipped her face up to his. Snow drifted onto her long, dark lashes, framing those rich chocolate eyes. Her unpainted mouth practically begged for affection as flakes melted against pale pink skin.

Damn it. That punch of lust to the gut was going to get him in trouble if he wasn't careful. He had a goal, and Zara was merely a stepping-stone. Harsh as that sounded, he had to remain fixed on the objective his late father had been adamant about—finding the family's lost heirlooms. Braden was near positive they were hidden somewhere inside Zara's house…a house that used to be in his family up until they lost everything in the Great Depression.

"You know, I can walk," she laughed, holding up her heels. "I swapped shoes, so I'm good."

"Maybe I'm holding on to you so *I* don't go down," he

retorted as he closed the door behind her and locked his vehicle. "I'll hold the light so you can get your keys out."

He kept an arm around her as they made fresh tracks to her back door. The snow was already well past their ankles, and the fat flakes continued to fall.

Zara pulled a set of keys from her coat pocket and gestured him into the house ahead of her. Once inside, she turned to the keypad and attempted to reset the alarm. With a shrug, Zara said, "Habit to come in and enter my code. Guess that's out, too."

Braden ran his light over the room, noticing how spacious the kitchen was and the wide, arched doorway leading into the living area. More light would be nice, now that he was actually inside. Somewhere his father was laughing at the irony of Braden finally getting in…and not being able to see a damn thing. But a power outage wasn't going to stop him from making use of this opportunity.

"Do you have flashlights and candles?" he asked, bringing his light back around but careful to keep it from shining in her eyes.

"I know where my candles are, but I'm not sure about the flashlights. I've only been here a few months. I haven't actually unpacked everything, yet." Zara removed her coat and hung it by the back door. "Let me hang your coat up since you're staying."

Braden removed his coat and started to hand it over when Zara reached out, her hand connecting with his cheek. "Oh, sorry. I didn't mean to punch you."

Braden welcomed the impact, as her fist caused no damage but reminded him that he needed to focus. "I'm fine," he stated as he maneuvered out of his coat while holding his light. "It's hard to see, so I'd say we'll be bumping into each other."

Not that he was complaining about the prospect of randomly brushing against her. Braden actually welcomed the friction. So long as he kept his goal in the forefront of his mind, bumping into Zara was definitely not a hardship.

"I know I have a candle in here and one on the coffee table in the living room. The matches are in the drawer beside the sink." She placed his coat on a hook beside hers. "I should try to figure out these gas logs in the living room first with the light of your phone."

She eased past him, her feet shuffling along the floor. Braden held his light over to where she was heading. Pulling open a drawer, Zara grabbed a box of matches before coming back to him.

She started forward but stopped. "You better stay close so you don't bump anything. I have several boxes in each room that are left from the move."

Stay close? No problem at all. Braden slid his hand around the dip in her waist and gave her a light squeeze as he leaned down to whisper in her ear. "How's this?"

Beneath his touch, her body trembled. Just the reaction he'd wanted…except now he was on the verge of trembling, too, because damn, she smelled so amazingly good and her silky hair tickled his lips. Wait, wasn't he the one who was supposed to be seducing? She wasn't even trying, and she nearly had him begging.

"Well, maybe not that close," she murmured as she attempted to put distance between them.

He moved with her, keeping their contact light so as not to freak her out right off the bat. Let her get used to his touch, his nearness. He planned on getting a whole lot closer.

"You realize this isn't a good idea?" she asked.

"Lighting the logs is the best idea. It's going to get colder in here if the electricity doesn't come back on."

Her soft laugh filled the darkness. "You know what I mean. I work for you."

"I'm aware of your position." With his hand on her waist,

Braden held his phone toward the living room. "I know we need to get heat in here, and if it's not with the logs, then we'll have to use a more…primal method."

Zara slowly started forward. "Acting on any desire because of the circumstances is a bad, bad idea for both of us."

"I've forgotten nothing, Zara." He allowed his body to move with hers, making sure to stay close. "Why don't we work on keeping warm and finding more sources of light? Then we can discuss the circumstances and what's going on between us."

Zara threw him a look over her shoulder. "We can settle this right now. I need this job and even if I was attracted to you—"

"Which you are."

"*If* I was," she countered in a louder tone to cut him off. "I wouldn't risk sleeping with you and damaging our working relationship."

He could barely make out her face in the darkness, and his light was facing ahead. But the way her body slightly leaned against his, the way she continued to tremble beneath his touch told him that her little speech was as much for her as it was for him. A slight obstacle but nothing he couldn't handle.

At first he'd been all about searching her home, and he still was, but there was no reason a little seducing couldn't come into play. He was an expert multitasker, and having Zara plus finding his family's heirlooms would be the icing on the proverbial cake.

After a fun romp and hopefully discovering his family's scrolls, Braden would be on his way, and she'd never even have to know his true intentions. Nobody would get hurt, and everything about this situation was legal. See? He did have a moral side, after all.

She could deny wanting him, but he was a master at lying and recognized that trait in others. So, let her think what she wanted…he knew the truth, and he'd completely use her attraction to his advantage.

"Fair enough," he told her. "I'll not mention it again."

That didn't mean he wouldn't touch her or seduce her with his actions. The darkness provided the perfect setting for seduction, but it could make it a bit harder to snoop. Granted, the darkness could also provide him the cover he needed to look without being seen.

So, as far as he understood, the nine scrolls, which had been in his family since his ancestor transcribed them from Shakespeare himself, were last known to be in this house. The history ran deep with his Irish family, and the precious scrolls were lost in the chaos of the fall of the O'Sheas during the 1930s. The trunk that had been recovered from this home after the Depression had shown up empty, so it only made sense the scrolls were here…somewhere.

Decades had passed, and Braden's family had attempted to purchase the property, but Zara's family had owned it since the O'Sheas lost it and they were adamant about not being bought.

Several attempts were made by Braden's father to purchase the place, but the efforts were always blocked. Eventually Patrick opted to go about things the illegal way. Ryker had even broken in a couple of times when Zara's grandmother had been alive. The old lady had been sharp, and Ryker had been forced to dodge the cops, but they were still left empty-handed. Patrick O'Shea had even mentioned waiting until the elderly lady passed and trying again to purchase the property, but Patrick had passed before Zara's grandmother.

So, Braden would get the job done himself. Failure was not an option, and buying the place wasn't necessary at this point.

Would the scrolls be somewhere obvious? Doubtful, or someone would've found them by now, and if those scrolls *had* been found, they would've made headlines around the world. His ancestor, a monk, had transcribed original works, supposedly plays that never came to be.

Zara sank to her knees in front of the fireplace. "Shine that light a little closer."

He did as requested, waiting while she fidgeted with getting the pilot light going.

"Need help?" he offered.

"Damn it." She sat back on her heels and shook her head. "This one isn't working. It was always causing Gram issues, but I'd assumed it was fixed. I know the unit in my bedroom works fine because I've used it."

Braden shouldn't delight in the fact her bedroom had gas heat and nowhere else in the house seemed to, but he was a guy, and, well, he couldn't help himself.

"Then maybe we should find those flashlights and more candles and head upstairs."

Zara threw him a look over her shoulder as she came to her feet and turned to fully face him. "Get that gleam out of your eye. I'm on to you."

Not yet she wasn't.

"What gleam?" he asked. "It's dark, so how can you see anything?"

"Oh, I can see enough and this can't get any more awkward than it already is."

"I'm not feeling awkward at all." He focused back on her eyes and offered a smile. "Are you?"

"Damn it, you know I am. Even if this—" she gestured between them "—wasn't making me nervous, you're my first overnight guest in this house."

Surprised, Braden shifted. "You mean Shane—damn. None of my business."

Zara crossed her arms over her chest. "After rescuing me tonight, I'd say this is your business. Shane never stayed here. We were dating when my grandmother passed, but he wasn't there for me much during that time. That's when I started reevaluating our relationship."

A pity Braden couldn't have gotten away with punching Shane in the face, but he hadn't wanted to cause any more of a scene at his home during the party. This was his first appearance as head of the family; he needed to hold tight to that power, that control.

What man wasn't there for his woman during a difficult time? Shane had always been a bit of a stuffed shirt, a man who probably polished his cuff links and didn't even know how to pleasure a woman properly. Braden knew for damn sure when he got Zara into bed, he'd know exactly what to do to her, with her and for her.

Seduction hadn't been a key factor in his grand scheme, but he wasn't looking the gift horse in the mouth. He couldn't deny the attraction, and why should he ignore such a strong pull?

"I don't want to talk about Shane." Zara maneuvered around him. "Let's go find the flashlights. I suppose you'll have to sleep in my room, but that is not an invitation to any other activity."

"I'll be a perfect gentleman." He'd have her begging before the night was over. "You won't have to worry about a thing." Except that he'd be snooping through her house once she fell asleep, and he'd be stealing back what was rightfully his.

Braden shone his light toward the steps and watched her head up. Like a predator after his prey, he followed those swaying hips snug in that killer dress. If he were totally honest with himself, he'd admit that Zara had the upper hand here. Even though she had no idea why she'd been hired and why he was so eager to be in her home, she had completely taken him by surprise with her professionalism, her kick-ass attitude and her sliver of vulnerability. She'd worked his party with a smile on her face and a firm hand where her assistants were concerned, all the while trying to keep Shane silenced and take on the difficult situation herself.

He tamped down his frustration. No personal emotions were allowed to creep in on his plan. A fling was all he'd allow.

He was on a mission, and Zara was in the crosshairs.

Three

Zara stepped into her bedroom, even more aware of the crackling intimacy. The intense stare Braden had offered, the way his eyes had darted to her lips more than once... she wasn't naive and she wasn't afraid of the rumors of him being such a bad boy.

Although he'd felt very bad in a delicious way when he'd been dancing with her earlier.

However, she was fully aware that he was her boss and no matter how much she ached for him to make a move, she knew anything beyond a professional relationship would be a mistake. Besides, she couldn't commit herself to anything other than a physical relationship with any man, so that definitely left Braden O'Shea out.

Zara suppressed a laugh as they stood just inside her bedroom. Yes, this was totally professional, especially since she had a stack of bras on her dresser she'd yet to put away. Thankfully he hadn't shone the light there yet. At least the unpacked boxes were lining her walk-in closet, so that was helpful.

"My room is the only one with a king bed, but I can sleep on the chaise and you can have the bed."

Her face flushed. Why had she said anything about a bed? Why talk about the elephant in the room? She'd been so worried about this situation becoming awkward, but she was the one making it worse. Clearly Braden wasn't nervous. And why should he be? He was well aware of how jittery she was, which only proved he held the upper hand here.

"I just meant that you're a big guy and you'd be more comfortable in my bed—er, a bigger bed." *Great, Zara. Keep babbling. When one foot goes in the mouth, throw the other one in, as well.*

Braden leaned against the door frame to her bedroom. With his light facing outward, she couldn't read the expression on his face.

"I'm making you nervous."

Clearly she wasn't convincing him that she was confident. "No... Maybe a little."

That low, rich laugh filled the bedroom, enveloping her in an awareness of just how intimate this situation was going to get, whether she wanted to admit it or not.

"Chemistry and attraction can often be misinterpreted as nerves."

Zara couldn't help but laugh. "Get off the attraction. I'm your employee, and your bold statements make this awkward."

"I see no reason not to be bold." He shifted, closing the gap slightly between them. "But I've promised not to bring up the matter again, so let's just focus on staying warm. It's late, and we both need sleep."

Really? He was just going to leave it at that? Maybe he was going to hold true to his word. Zara was almost disappointed, but she shouldn't be. Braden had to be strong, because if he continued to make remarks or advances, she didn't know how long her self-control would hold out.

Hopefully the roads would be better tomorrow, and Braden could go home. Then this would all be a memory, and they would move on with their working relationship. Because that's what they should do, right? He had another party coming up in a few months, and since she'd been hired as the O'Sheas' permanent events coordinator, she had to keep her mind focused on her career.

"I'll hold the light," he told her. "Let's get these logs on."

After the logs were on and heat started filling the room, then they went in search of more flashlights, and Zara grabbed her cell. She had almost a full battery and she hoped it held out until the electricity came back on. If need be, she could always charge it in his car if the electricity stayed off too long.

Unfortunately, the snow was still coming down just as fierce as it had been, and with the roads being a hazard, Zara had no doubt it would be a while before crews could work on the lines.

Mother Nature clearly had it out for her. First the roads, now the electricity. Throw in some darkness and watch that sexual tension skyrocket and blow their clothes off.

Zara cringed. No. The clothes had to stay on. They were her only shield of defense because she'd already imagined her boss naked, and if he actually took that suit off, she would not be responsible for her actions.

Once back in her bedroom, Braden closed the door to keep the heat in. Zara had lit a candle and sat it on her nightstand. The flickering, warm glow sent the room to a level of romance that had no business being here.

And then the fact that she was still wearing her black dress hit her. Great. So much for keeping all the clothes on.

"Um, I'm going to have to change." She hated how her tone sounded apologetic. This was her house, damn it. "I don't have anything to offer you unless you can fit in a pair of small sweatpants and one of my T-shirts."

"I'll be fine. Go, get out of that dress."

Those words combined with that sexy tone of his had her sighing. He'd promised not to mention sex, but the man practically oozed it with every action, every word.

"Can you wait in the hall for a second?" she asked.

Taking his own flashlight, Braden stepped out and closed the door behind him.

Zara quickly shoved her bras into her drawer and whipped her snug dress over her head. She peeled off her stockings and tossed them into a drawer, too. She really wanted to lose the bra, but she couldn't get that comfortable with her sexy guest.

As she pulled on a pair of leggings and an oversize sweatshirt, Zara truly wished she'd met Braden under different circumstances. Maybe then they could explore this attraction, but she couldn't risk intimacy when she needed this job, this recognition too much. She'd only had her grandmother, and now she was gone. There was no husband, no other family to fall back on if her financial world crumbled. Her company was only a year old, and being tied to the O'Sheas would launch her into a new territory of clientele.

Yes, the rumors of O'Shea's Auction House being the front for illegal activity had been abuzz for years—decades, even—but the mystery surrounding the family only kept people more intrigued, so Zara would gladly ride the coattails of their popularity.

After sliding on a pair of fuzzy socks and pulling her hair into a ponytail, Zara opened the door. Braden was texting but glanced up at her and slid his phone back into his pocket.

"I had to check in with the security team. I try to keep them updated on my whereabouts."

"Oh, you don't have to explain yourself."

"You look…different."

With a shrug, Zara glanced down to her outfit. "This is me in my downtime. I'm pretty laid-back."

Why did the room seem so much smaller when he came back in from the hallway? Why did he have such a presence about him that demanded attention? And how the hell did she act? What was the proper protocol for bringing your billionaire boss to your house and then having him spend the night? Milk and cookies? Bourbon and a cigar? She honestly didn't know the man on a personal level.

Zara's cell vibrated on her dresser. With the screen facing down, she didn't see the caller before she picked it up and automatically slid her finger over the screen.

"Hello?"

"Hey, I wanted to make sure you made it home okay."

"Shane."

Zara's eyes darted to Braden. In the dim light she could see his narrowed gaze, his jaw clenched.

"I know I acted like a jerk earlier, but I want another chance with you and I was worried about you getting home in this storm."

Were his words slurring?

"Shane, it's nearly one in the morning. Are you drunk?"

He must've shifted, because there was the slightest bit of static coming through the phone before he continued. "I miss you, Zara."

She turned her back to Braden and rubbed her forehead. "I got home safe. Thanks for checking, but we really are over, Shane. Good night."

"Don't hang up." Now his voice rose, as if the real Shane was emerging. "You're selfish, you know that? I'm trying to talk to you, and you're already dismissing me. We were good together, you know it."

"No, we weren't, and I'm done with—"

Suddenly the phone was ripped from her hand. Zara whirled around as Braden hit the end button and then turned the phone off.

"You won't explain yourself to him."

Zara sighed. Damn it, why did he have to be right? "He's not been this persistent until the past week or so. I'm not sure why he wants to get back together so bad, but I swear he won't affect my work with you."

Braden closed the gap between them and stared down at her. The darkness slashing over half his face made him seem even more menacing, more intriguing.

"I don't give a damn about that. I know you're a professional. But I'm not going to stand here and listen to you defend yourself to an asshole who doesn't deserve you."

"Wow." Zara crossed her arms and tried to process Braden's words, his angry tone. "Um…thanks."

Unsure what to do next, Zara glanced around the room. "I guess I'll just grab a blanket and pillow and lie down. I'm pretty beat."

The strain of the evening had seriously taken its toll on her, and all she wanted to do was crawl on to her chaise and fall dead asleep. Okay, maybe that wasn't all she wanted to do, but doing her boss was out of the question.

By the time she'd gotten situated on the chaise, she glanced to her bed where Braden sat on the edge staring in her direction.

"What?"

"Are you going to be comfortable? I didn't expect to take your bed."

Seeing him there, knowing her sheets would smell like him long after he was gone, was just another layer of arousal she didn't need.

"I'm perfectly comfortable. You're the one still in a suit."

With a soft laugh, he shook his head. In moments, he had his jacket off and was in the process of unbuttoning his shirt.

"Uh, wait. Are you undressing? Because—"

"Zara." His hands froze on the buttons. "I'm just taking my shirt off."

Just taking his shirt off. *To which he will no doubt ex-*

pose a chest she'll want to stare at. With the light from the gas fireplace and the candle on the nightstand, she could see perfectly fine.

And yup. He'd taken his black dress shirt off and revealed an amazingly sculpted chest, smattered with dark hair and…was that ink on his arm?

"You're staring," he said without looking up at her. "You're going to make me blush."

Zara laughed. "I highly doubt you blush, let alone over a woman looking at you." Because why deny the fact she had been? She'd been caught, but she didn't care. The man was worth a good, long stare. "Good night, Braden."

Her damn floral scent mocked him as he lay on top of her plush comforter. With his hands laced behind his head, Braden stared up at the ceiling watching the orange flickering glow from the candle. He wouldn't get any sleep tonight. Besides the fact he had every intention of getting back up to check out the house after Zara had gone to sleep, how the hell could he actually rest when the object of his desire was lying only feet away?

He hadn't expected to actually want her with such a passion and fierceness. Damn it. He knew he'd been attracted, but he'd passed being attracted long ago. Now he had a need so deeply embedded within him, he was going to go mad if he didn't have her.

Zara had been knockout gorgeous in that black dress and those sexy heels earlier at his party. But seeing her in such a simple, natural way, with hair up and sweats on, had Braden questioning why the hell he wasn't coercing her into this giant bed. He could have her clothes off in record time, despite what she'd said about mixing business and pleasure. The allure was there—the chemistry was hot enough to scorch them.

But he had a mission. One that couldn't be forgotten just because he'd been sidetracked by this unexpected quest for Zara. He needed to focus. Sex was one thing, a marvelous thing actually, but she'd put up a defensive wall. He was alone in the house he'd been wanting in for quite some time. So why the hell was he lying here focused on what was denied to him instead of formulating a plan of where he'd search once she was fully asleep?

Braden suppressed a groan as he rolled to his side. He needed to start this process, so he could be ready to get the hell out when the roads cleared.

The scrolls had to be in this house. They had to be; he refused to believe any different. But at the same time, he had to be realistic. His family had lost this house and everything in it during the Great Depression—a little fact Zara most likely didn't know.

In the decades that had passed, who's to say someone hadn't found the scrolls, moved them to another location and kept the secret to themselves?

A gnawing pit formed in his stomach. What if someone had found them and thought they were trash?

No, the scrolls were supposedly rolled up in small tubes. Nine different tubes for the nine works. They were somewhere, and Braden wasn't going to leave this house until he'd searched every inch of it.

He thought of the built-in bookcases in the living room he'd spotted earlier when he'd ran his phone light over the room. He'd tried to be casual about it, no reason to raise a red flag with Zara, because, as of right now, she was totally unsuspecting and completely worried about being alone with him.

Since she'd walked into his office for the job, he knew he wanted her in his bed. No reason he couldn't enjoy a little recreational activity and search at the same time. Besides, getting Zara to open up to him may be the angle they'd needed all along, even if Ryker just wanted to break in and be done with it.

No way in hell was Ryker getting close to Zara. He was

mysterious at best, terrifying at worst. And women loved that mysterious side. He had no intention of Zara being one of those women. Zara was all Braden's...for now.

Braden knew full well what Ryker did for the family. Ever since Ryker had come to be friends with Braden and Mac in grade school, their father had taken Ryker in as another son. By the time they were out of high school, Ryker was just another member of the family. The Black Sheep was too benign a term when referring to the man who did all the dirty work.

Braden stared across to Zara and realized she was looking right back at him. This was ridiculous. They were adults acting like horny teens trying to get a mental feel for what the other one was thinking.

"You're supposed to be asleep," he told her. "Do you need your bed back?"

The image of Zara in her bed wasn't new. He didn't need to say the words aloud to conjure up a vivid image. He'd already had her in bed several times in his mind.

"I can't sleep."

He knew a cure for insomnia.

"It's too quiet," she continued. "I usually sleep with a fan because I can't handle the silence at night."

Interesting. Braden bent his elbow and rested his head on his palm. "Are you afraid to stay here alone?"

"Not really. It's just my old place was so much smaller, and this house has always had that creepy factor, you know? It's old, it creaks and groans. Then there's the rumor it's haunted." She laughed. "I guess when I'm alone with my thoughts, I let my imagination run wild."

"It's not unusual for these old homes to have some ghost story. They're either based off some truth people believe, or they make for a good resale value for those seeking adventure."

"Yeah, well, I'm not up for an adventure and I don't believe in ghosts."

Braden found he liked hearing her talk. He liked how soft her voice was, how it carried through the darkness and hit him straight with a shot of arousal. So he wanted to keep her talking.

"Since we both can't sleep, why don't you tell me the ghost story?"

He saw her lick her lips as she clutched the blanket near her chest. Thanks to the dim lighting, Braden found her even more alluring. Sleep wasn't even a priority.

"It's silly, actually. Apparently there was a young couple in love, and supposedly the man went off to the army and never returned. There are stories he died in the war, stories he fell in love with another. Who knows? She went on to marry, but the rumor is you can still hear her crying."

Braden knew that story all too well. Considering this house had been in his family at the time Zara was referring to. And the woman was his great-great…several greats, grandmother. He'd always heard the story that the man who went to the army was actually her husband and he'd been killed. She'd remarried, had children but, supposedly, never got over her first love. A tragic story, a romantic one for those who were into that sort of thing…and his Irish family most definitely was.

"But, if I ever hear a woman crying in this house, it will take me one giant leap to get out of here," Zara went on with a light laugh. "An intruder I can handle. A ghost, not so much. At least a real person I can shoot."

The more she talked, the more Braden found he didn't like her in this big house alone. But, if she had a firearm, at least she could defend herself.

What if Shane showed up? The man obviously called her drunk, and, on a good night with clear roads, what would stop him from just coming over, forcing his way in? And now that she worked for Braden, Shane would see that as a betrayal. The man was that egotistical and warped.

"But I'm not sure a woman would be crying over a man

if she was married to another," Zara went on as she shifted beneath her covers. "I mean, I can't imagine loving one man, let alone falling in love twice. Or maybe she'd just married the second guy so she wasn't lonely. I'll never be that desperate."

Braden thought to his parents. They'd been in love, they'd raised a family and they'd had a bond that Braden wanted to have someday. His mother passed when Braden had been a pre-teen, and the car accident that claimed her had an impact on the entire family. They became stronger, more unified than before because they realized just how short life was.

Not now, but one day he'd have a family of his own. First, though, he'd have those scrolls back in his family's possession and steer his family right. He refused to bring a family into his life when there were enemies, people who used loved ones as a weakness to exploit.

"You've never been in love? Never knew people in love?" he asked, easing up to rest his back against the headboard.

"I've never seen love firsthand, no." Zara turned onto her back, lacing her hands on top of the blanket. "My grandmother loved me and I loved her, but as far as a man and woman... I'm not sure true love exists. Have you been in love?"

Even though he'd removed everything but his pants, heat enveloped Braden. Granted, it could be because he was in the company of a woman he wanted more than his next breath, but honestly, the logs were doing a great job, and with the door closed, the thick air was starting to become too much.

"Would you mind if I turned the logs down a bit?" he asked.

"Nice way to dodge my question." She jumped up from the chaise and threw him a smile. "I'll turn them down. It is getting a bit warm in here."

Braden watched her move across the room. In her black, body-hugging dress she'd been a knockout, but in her sweatshirt and leggings with her hair in a ponytail, she almost seemed...innocent, vulnerable.

Damn it, he didn't want to see her that way. He didn't want this to become personal with emotions getting in the way of his quest to get her in his bed and search for the scrolls.

And when the hell had he officially added her to his list of must-haves?

Somewhere between dancing with her and settling in for their sleepover.

As she started back to the chaise, she gestured toward him. "If you're hot, you can, um...you can take your pants off. I won't look. I mean, I don't want this to be uncomfortable for either of us, but I want you to be... Sorry, I'm rambling. Go ahead, take your pants off. I'll turn around."

She was killing him. Slowly, surely, killing him.

But the lady said he could remove his pants. So remove them he would.

Four

Just as Braden unzipped and started to lower his pants, Zara cried out in pain, followed quickly by words that would've made his mama blush.

With pants hanging open, Braden carefully crossed the space. "What is it?"

"Banged the side of my ankle on this damn chaise," she said through gritted teeth. "Stupid scrolled legs on this thing."

Without thinking, Braden dropped to his knees before her. His hands ran down the leg closest to the chaise, gently roaming over her tight, knit pants.

When she hissed, he pulled back and glanced up. The light was even dimmer now that she'd turned the logs down, but the miniscule candle flickered just enough of a glow for him to make out those heavy lids and the desire that stared back at him.

Keeping his eyes locked on to hers, Braden slid his fingers around her slender ankle once again. "Does this hurt?"

"Just tender."

Trailing his fingertips to another spot, he asked, "How about here?"

"No."

Weighing his next movement, Braden moved his hand on up to her calf. Zara sucked in a breath, and he knew it was for a whole other reason. Gliding over the back of her knee, he curled his hands around her thigh as he shifted closer to her. With his other hand, he slid beneath the hem of her sweatshirt to grip her waist. Satiny skin met his palm, and he'd swear she trembled and broke out in goose bumps right that second.

"Braden," she murmured.

"Relax."

Ironic he was telling her to relax when his own body was strung tighter than a coil ready to spring into action.

"This isn't appropriate," she whispered. If her tone had held any conviction whatsoever, he would've stopped, but with the way she'd panted his name, with the way her hips slightly tilted toward him, he wasn't about to ignore what her body was so obviously telling him.

He continued to allow his hands the freedom to roam as he came to his feet, pulling her with him. With one hand settled on her hip and one just beneath her shirt, he watched as Zara stared up at him, her eyes locked on to his. He refused to break the connection, didn't want to sever the intensity of this moment.

That warm skin begged for his touch, and it was all Braden could do not to jerk this shirt up and over her head so he could fully appreciate the woman. The seduction of Zara would have to be slow, romantic and all about her. He could handle that order because right now he wanted to feel her, wanted to have her come apart.

The second he encountered silk over her breast, he wasted no time in reaching around and unfastening her bra. Now that she was freed of the restraint, he cupped both breasts in his palms and watched with utter satisfaction as her lids drifted closed, as a groan escaped from her lips.

Why did she have to feel so amazing? Why was he fighting taking what he wanted instead of giving her full pleasure? This had to be about Zara, about seduction.

Braden slid one hand down to the top of her pants. Zara's eyes snapped open. She scrambled from beneath his touch. Her eyes darted away as she righted her clothes. Damn it, he'd pushed her too far when he couldn't control his hormones.

"This can't happen," she stated, her voice shaky. "We—I…"

"Don't say you're sorry," he told her as she jerked her sweatshirt down as if she was trying to erase what had just occurred. "We're adults, and dancing around the attraction wasn't going to last for long. I've been wanting to touch you since you walked into my office."

Zara's hands came up to her face. "I can't believe I did that. I just let you…" She dropped her hands and waved them in the air. "I let you…"

"Yes?" he asked, trying not to smile as she struggled.

"Is this how you treat all your new employees?"

Braden reached for her arms, pulling her flush against his body. "I've never in my life slept with an employee."

"We haven't slept together," she retorted.

"Yet."

Her gasp had him laughing, but he didn't release her. "You're so sure of yourself, aren't you? I'm not easy, Braden. I don't want you to even think that for a minute. I shouldn't have let this go so far."

"Zara, if I thought you were easy, I wouldn't waste my time trying. I look for the challenge, the chase, the risk in everything."

Now she laughed as she shook her head. Her hands were trapped between their bodies. "You're already talking about sleeping with me and you've not even kissed me. I'd say that's—"

His lips slammed on to hers. Hadn't kissed her? Was she complaining?

For one troubling moment, Braden worried she'd push him away, but after her hesitancy, she finally opened up and accepted what he was giving.

Her hands flattened against his chest as he coaxed her mouth open and tipped her head. Kissing Zara was just another total-body experience he hadn't anticipated. Kisses were either good or bad. With Zara, they were arousing, a stepping-stone for more and a promise of all the passion she kept hidden away.

If he wasn't careful, he'd start craving more of her touches, more of her soft moans, because damn it, the woman got into a man's system and…

No. Hell, no. She was not getting into his system. Nobody was penetrating that until he was damn good and ready.

Braden had to force himself to step back, to put some distance between their heated bodies.

"There. Now you've been kissed." He licked his own lips, needing to taste her again. "If you're feeling cheated on anything else, I can oblige."

Her eyes widened as she trailed her gaze down his bare chest. "N-no. You've obliged enough."

Braden smiled. "Then we both need to get some sleep."

As if he hadn't just had her body trembling against his seconds ago, he turned and sat back on her bed. Zara hadn't moved from her spot next to the chaise.

"Is your ankle okay?"

"My ankle?" She glanced down. "Oh, yeah. It's sore, but fine. Um…good night."

He watched as she slowly sank down onto her makeshift bed. He could practically hear her thinking and he knew full well she was replaying how far she'd let him go. Hell, he was, too, but he had to push that aside and keep his eye on the main reason he was here and not how close he'd been to getting her to explode in his arms.

"Don't overthink this, Zara." She continued to lie there, looking up at the ceiling. "Get some sleep."

Because the sooner she fell asleep, the quicker he could start looking through the house.

How could the man just fall asleep? Seriously? Braden acted as if this was no big deal, as if he'd patted her on the head and sent her off to bed like an obedient lover.

And the longer she lay here, the more she was wondering how she'd lost control of that situation so fast. Oh, yeah. He'd touched her. That was it. The man touched her, looked at her with those piercing eyes, and she'd been helpless. For the briefest of moments she'd forgotten all about her job, the fact her boss had his hands beneath her shirt and was working his way into her pants. Thankfully, she'd come to her senses before they'd crossed a point of no return. She needed this job, even more than she needed a one-night stand.

Braden O'Shea was a powerful man, and she was not immune to his allure. Yet she'd told herself over and over this evening how she couldn't get intimate with him, no matter how much she wanted to. She couldn't risk losing this job because she was a sad cliché and slept with her boss. How tacky was that? She prided herself on being a professional, yet the man who'd written her a colossal check was snoozing in her bed.

Whatever his secret for flipping the horny switch, she'd like to know because she was still just as turned on as before she'd put the brakes on.

She'd never known a man who was so giving, but then she hadn't known many men like Braden O'Shea. Something told her he was quite different than any other guy she'd dated.

Zara nearly groaned as she tugged on her blanket and rolled over. Dated? She and Braden were far from dating.

He'd given her a few minutes of toe-curling excitement, and that was all. He was stuck in her house thanks to Mother Nature's fury, and that was the extent of their personal relationship.

From here on out, no more touching, no more kissing. Though she had to admit that kiss had been nearly as potent as the touching.

What would morning bring? The questions whirled around in her head. Would he act as if nothing happened? Would he be able to leave, or would he be stuck here for another night? Zara wished he weren't her boss, wished this powerful, sexy man were stuck in her house under different circumstances, but the fact was he was helping to pay her bills. And without the prestige of working for him, it would take her a lot longer to get the recognition she needed for her new company.

She wasn't worried about his questionable reputation. The O'Sheas were legends, and despite the rumors surrounding Braden's father's dealings, Zara had only heard praise about Braden. He may be tough when needed, he may even show off his brute force like he had with Shane, but none of that made him a bad guy. And the way her body was still thrumming, Zara felt Braden was indeed a very good guy.

No matter what her common sense was telling her now, Zara couldn't help but want more. Not being able to touch Braden at all left her feeling somewhat cheated. Those broad shoulders, those lean hips…a man with a body like that surely knew how to use it in the most effective ways.

Gripping her blanket beneath her chin, Zara tried not to think about the man who lay just behind her, in her bed, shirtless. She tried not to think of how he'd looked at her when he'd been kneeling on the floor. She tried to keep her body from tingling even more at the fantasy of how they'd be if she crawled in between those sheets with him.

Her best hope now would be to fall asleep and dream, because having the real thing was simply out of the question.

Braden padded from the bedroom. It had taken Zara over an hour to fall asleep. She'd tossed and turned, letting out soft little moans every now and then, and there wasn't a doubt in Braden's mind she was just as sexually frustrated as he was.

Zara was one of the most passionate women he'd ever met. And when she let her guard down...purely erotic. Knowing she was lying over there restless nearly had him forgetting the plan to search the house tonight and instead dragging her back up to her own bed and finishing what they both wanted.

But she'd finally dozed off, if the subtle snoring was any indication. Braden threw one more look her way as he gently closed the door behind him. The logs were keeping the room plenty warm, because this hallway was flat-out chilly. The temperature must have really dropped outside for the inside to get so cold, so fast. At least he'd put his shirt and socks back on, so that was a minor help.

With his phone in his pocket, Braden flicked on the small flashlight that had been on Zara's bedside table. He swung it back and forth down the hallway, finally deciding to venture into the rooms toward the end where he'd never been before.

He'd seen the layout of the home several times. The floor plan was ingrained into his mind, the blueprints locked away in his home office, but seeing the rooms firsthand was entirely different. He knew there was a third floor, but right now he was going to focus on the bedrooms that sat empty. Every inch of this home could be a hiding spot, and Braden had to start somewhere. Sticking close to Zara was the smartest move right now.

There was something eerie about an old house that was pitch-black with the sounds of whirling winds and creaking. But fear never entered Braden's mind. Nothing scared him, except the prospect of not finding these scrolls. His father had wanted them back in the family's possession, but once Patrick had passed away six months ago, Braden knew this endeavor now fell to him. That, and strategically severing the ties to an underbelly of the city he wanted nothing to do with.

Nearly a decade ago, his father had supposedly ordered a prominent businessman to be taken out, along with the man's assistant. That dangerous rumor kept filtering around, but if Braden could pull this family around, point them in the right direction, perhaps such whispered speculations would be put to rest.

Everything would take time. This was a business Braden learned to be patient in. Effective, forceful and controlling, but patient.

He'd never ordered any killings, prayed to God he never had to. Transitioning was difficult, but Braden had to. He had to secure a future for the family he eventually wanted, but at the same time fulfill his father's dying wishes.

As he entered the last bedroom, he stood in the doorway and moved his light around, familiarizing himself with the furniture layout. More built-in bookcases. Nice charm to add to each room, but a pain in the ass for someone on a scavenger hunt.

Ryker had mentioned searching the obvious places, but Braden was here now and wanted to see everything for himself firsthand.

Braden slid the flashlight beneath his arm so he could use both hands to shift books and knickknacks around on the shelves. So far no hidden door, no secret hole hidden behind a panel. Nothing. But he wasn't discouraged. Getting into this house was one of the biggest hurdles, and here he was. Now he just needed to be patient, because the scrolls were here. They had to be.

The irony that his family unofficially dealt in retrieving stolen relics and heirlooms, and they couldn't even get back their own possessions, was not lost on him. Granted, they technically stole back the items, but those words would never come out of his mouth, and Ryker was the guy who did all the dirty work. So in a sense, Braden never saw how the items were taken back. So long as it was done correctly and satisfied clients all over the globe, the details didn't matter. The auction house gave them the front they needed to play modern-day Robin Hood, but the rumors around the family gave them that edge that helped them with their tough, hard-ass image.

Generations of corruption would be hard to move past, but Braden was determined. The art dealings would continue, and there was no harm in taking back what was rightfully due to those who had lost heirlooms, as long as it didn't require any violence. But any more than lying and stealing had to cease…sooner rather than later.

Ryker wasn't too keen on Braden's new, somewhat lilywhite direction, but Braden wasn't asking for permission. He was in charge now, and Ryker would have to understand that any sort of bloodshed was a thing of the past.

Which reminded him, he needed to check in with their right-hand man who was currently in London looking for a rare piece of art that needed to be returned to a client in Paris during the next auction.

By the time he'd finished the two large bedrooms at the end of the hall, Braden was no closer than when he'd started. Sleep was going to have to happen because his eyes were burning, and most likely it was nearly morning at this point. He couldn't help but wonder what all the unpacked boxes were, though. He'd seen a few in her kitchen, several in the living room, and with her closet door open, he'd spotted a good amount stacked in there. Hadn't she said she'd lived here for a few months?

Those unpacked boxes held so much potential, but how many were hers and how many were already here for years?

Using his flashlight to head back to the bedroom, Braden

flicked it off as soon as he reached the doorway. The second he stepped inside, warmth surrounded him. Zara lay on her side, her hand tucked beneath her cheek, her ponytail now in disarray as hair draped over her forehead and down the side of her face.

Slipping back out of his shirt, he sat on the edge of the bed, unable to take his eyes off the sleeping beauty. He had tried to keep his hands off her. Okay, he could've tried harder, but damn it, something about her made him want to get closer to her in the most primal way possible.

He knew she was a sexy, take-charge woman. The fact she was a businesswoman, career-driven and independent, was a definite turn-on. But after dancing with her and seeing that flash of vulnerability in her eyes when Shane had entered the picture, Braden felt even more territorial…and not in the typical employee/employer way. There was no way he could not step into her life.

Braden slid between the sheets and refused to acknowledge the arousal threatening to keep him awake. He needed sleep because when morning came, he fully intended to continue his quest for the scrolls, and he sure as hell planned on more seducing. Multitasking had never been this sweet.

Five

Zara stared at her cabinets and sighed. Was it appropriate to offer your millionaire boss a s'mores Pop-Tart or a cherry one for breakfast? Because that was the extent of her options. Well, she had other flavors because she was a junk-food junkie, and Pop-Tarts were her drug of choice.

He'd still been asleep when she'd slipped from the warm room. Now she stood shivering in her kitchen and wondering when the electricity would be restored. The snow was still coming down in big, fat flakes, and there was no sign of any cars in sight.

Grabbing three different varieties of breakfast pastries, Zara spun on her fuzzy socks and raced back up the steps. Mercy, it had gotten cold in here. When she eased open the door, Braden was shifting around on her bed, sheets slipping down a bit. His glorious chest looked even better with daylight streaking through the window. Granted, it had also looked spectacular on display with the fire flickering last night.

With boxes of food under one arm, she gently closed the door behind her, but Braden's eyes instantly popped open and zeroed in on her. Suddenly she was pinned in place. That piercing gaze penetrated her across the room. Such a potent man to be able to hold such power over someone without even saying a word.

Slowly, he sat up. The sheet fell to his waist, giving up an even more tantalizing view of all that tan skin with dark hair covering his chest. Dark ink curved over one shoulder, and Zara found herself wanting to trace the lines of that tat. With her tongue.

Down, girl.

"Breakfast," she said. "I hope you like Pop-Tarts."

His brows drew in. "I can honestly say I've never had one."

Of course he hadn't. Not only was he a bajillionaire, he had the body of a sculpted god. Someone who looked like that wouldn't fill themselves with the finer junkie things in life.

"Well, you're in for a treat." She crossed the room, trying to ignore the fact that she looked like a hot mess after last night. "I'm a connoisseur of all things unhealthy and amazingly tasty."

She sat the boxes on the trunk at the end of her bed and opened each one. She tried to focus on anything other than the fact he still hadn't reached for his shirt. Was he going to spend their entire time half naked? So this is what the saying "both a blessing and a curse" meant.

"I have s'mores, cherry and chocolate." She glanced back up as he slid from the bed and came to stand beside her. "Take whatever you want. I have plenty more downstairs."

He eyed the boxes as if he truly had no clue what to choose. "I'm a chocolate lover, so the cherry is out. Should I go all in for the s'mores?"

Zara smiled. "They're the best, in my opinion."

She handed him a foil package and grabbed one for herself before heading over to stand near the logs. She needed to keep a bit of distance, because if the shirtless thing wasn't enough to make her want a replay of last night, the fact that he had sheet marks—*her* sheets—on his arm and face and he smelled musky and sexy was more than enough to have her near begging. And Zara wouldn't beg for any man, especially one who wrote her checks.

"You can have all you want, though." She was babbling. Nerves did that to a woman. "I forgot the drinks. I'm sure the fridge kept things cold, but I'll need to—"

"Zara. Breathe." Braden's hand gripped her shoulder. She hadn't even heard him come up behind her. "I'm making you nervous again."

Swallowing, she turned to face him. Holding his heavy-lidded gaze, Zara tried not to look at the sheet mark on his cheek. A minor imperfection that made this man seem so... normal.

"I'm not nervous," she said, defensively. "Why would I be nervous? I mean, just because you... I...last night...and now your shirt is still off, so I'm not sure what to do or how to act. I've never had a man here, let alone my boss. So this whole morning-after thing is different, not that we did anything to discuss the typical morning after..."

Closing her eyes, Zara let out a sigh. She shook her head to clear her thoughts before looking back up to Braden. "I'm rambling. This is just a bit awkward for me, and I didn't want to make a total fool of myself, but I'm doing just that."

Braden took the package from her hands and tore it open. After pulling out a Pop-Tart, he held it up to her.

"Why don't you eat?" he suggested. "I'm not worried about what happened last night, but if you want to run through it again, that's fine with me. Maybe we can discuss how much farther I wanted to go."

"No, we shouldn't." Zara took the pastry he held up to her. "Maybe we should just check on the road conditions instead of reliving anything."

Braden laughed as he tore open his own package. "Whatever you want. I'm at your mercy here."

Did every word that came out of his mouth have to drip with sex appeal? Was he trying to torment her further? Because if this was him putting forth no effort to torture her, she'd hate to see when he actually turned on the charm.

Zara didn't want to think about staying in this room with him for another day. If she didn't get out of here, her hormones may explode.

They ate their gourmet breakfast, and Braden muttered something about them being amazing before he went and grabbed a different flavor. Traditional chocolate this time. While he had round two, Zara went to dig out her old boots. She was going to have to get the frozen food outside and put it into the snow to stay cold. There was no other way, not if she wanted to salvage her groceries.

After she shoved her fuzzy-socked feet into her boots, Zara headed for the door. "I'll be right back."

Braden swallowed his last bite and crumbled his foil in his hand. "Where are you going?"

"I'm going to run downstairs and get the food from the freezer and fridge and set it out in the snow. It will stay cold there. I don't know what else to do with it."

Crossing to the bed, Braden reached for his shirt and shrugged into it. "I'll help."

"You don't have to. I've got it."

Ignoring her, he buttoned each button with quick, precise movements. "What else do I have to do?"

Keep that potent, sexually charged body away from hers? Stay in the warm room while she went outside and cooled off?

Zara knew she wasn't going to win this argument, so she turned and headed from the room. Braden closed the bedroom door behind them. The cooler air in the hallway slid right through Zara, helping her to focus on something other than the man who pretended like make out sessions were passed out each night before bedtime like a hug good-night.

Should her body still be humming, given they hadn't even gotten to the good part? Seriously?

As soon as she went into the kitchen, she turned to Braden, only he wasn't there. Zara backtracked a couple steps to find him in the living room staring at the built-in bookcases.

"This house has a lot of the same old-Boston charm mine does," he told her without turning around. "The trim on the top of these cabinets, the detailed edging. It's all so rare to find in homes these days. I appreciate when properties have been taken care of."

"I imagine you see quite a variety of homes with various decor in your line of work."

Throwing her a glance over his shoulder, he nodded. "I've seen million-dollar homes that were polished to perfection, every single thing in them brand-new. But it's the old houses that really pull me in. Mac is more the guy who wants all things shiny and new."

Zara crossed her arms to ward off the chill. The only vibe she'd gotten of the younger O'Shea brother was that he was a player. And with his looks and charm, she could totally see women batting their lashes and dropping their panties.

Braden ran a fingertip over a small glass church her grandmother had loved. "He's working on the opening of our Miami location. That fast-paced lifestyle and the warmer climate are also more his speed."

"You guys are quite opposite, then."

"Except when it comes to business," Braden amended as he moved to another shelf and carefully adjusted a pewter picture frame holding a picture of Zara as a child. "We see eye to eye on all things regarding the auction house."

"I've always hated that picture," Zara stated with a laugh. "My grandmother took that on my first trip to the beach.

I was eleven and had just entered that awkward stage girls go through."

Turning to face her, Braden crossed his arms and offered a slight grin. "Whatever phase you went through, you've more than made up for it."

Zara shivered at his smooth words. Apparently this smooth talker liked a woman with curves.

"You didn't go to a beach until you were eleven?" he asked, moving right on.

Oh, no. She didn't want to get into her childhood. Granted, the first decade of her life wasn't terrible, but there certainly were no family vacations, no fun beach pictures or pictures of any kind, really. Her parents had been rich, beyond rich, but they couldn't buy affection. They'd tried. Zara had more toys, more nannies than any one child needed or deserved.

When her parents had died, Zara had been numb. She hadn't even known how to feel, how to react. How did a child respond to losing the two people who were supposed to love her more than anything, yet had never said the words aloud? They'd shown her in ways, material ways, but that was the only way they knew how to express themselves.

That money she'd always thought her parents possessed was suddenly gone. Her parents' overspending had finally caught up with them, and Zara was paying the price. Apparently her parents owed everybody and their brother thousands, if not hundreds of thousands. Zara's grandmother had maneuvered funds, had borrowed against this house and had paid off every last debt her parents had left. Now the money was gone after all the debts were paid.

Just another reason Zara was determined to succeed in her business. She wanted to make her grandmother proud, even if she wasn't here to physically see Zara's triumph. She didn't want to have to sell this house that had been in her family since the Depression. Her grandmother had loved this place, and Zara wanted that last piece of family to hold on to.

"Zara?" Braden took a cautious step toward her, then another. "Where did you go?"

Zara shook her head. "Nowhere worth traveling to again. Let's get this food outside and get back upstairs. I'm freezing."

Just as she turned, Braden curled his fingers around her arm. With a glance from his hand to his eyes, Zara thought she saw a flash of something other than the desire she'd seen previously. Those piercing eyes were now filled with concern, and Zara didn't want him to be concerned for her. Having compassion was just another level of intimacy she couldn't afford to slide into with this man. It would be all too easy to lean on someone, and she'd not been raised to be dependent on others.

Zara didn't want to identify the feelings coursing through her, not when her emotions were already on edge and her body hummed even louder each time he neared, let alone touched her.

"Come on, Braden." She forced a wide smile and nodded toward the kitchen. "Let's get this done."

He looked as if he wanted to say more, but finally he nodded and released her. Maybe if they could focus on food, not freezing to death and no conversations involving personal issues, they'd get through this blizzard without any more sensual encounters or touching.

As she plucked her coat from the peg by the back door, Zara nearly laughed at her delusional thought. No way could she pretend Braden being here was just like having a friend over. Where he'd gripped her arm seconds ago was still tingling, and in a very short time, she'd find herself back upstairs, closed off in her bedroom with a man who made her ache for things she had no business wanting.

"That's all of it." Milk, eggs, cheese, frozen pizzas, meat and other groceries were tucked down into the snow to keep them from going bad. "Let's get back inside before my toes fall off."

Even though she had her fuzzy socks on under her rubber boots, her toes were going numb.

Braden held up a hand. "Wait," he whispered. "Did you hear that?"

Zara stilled. All she heard was silence because no cars were out. It was as if the rest of the world had ceased to exist, leaving only her and the boss she'd dreamed of last night.

"I don't hear anything," she told him, shoving that fantasy aside. "You have to be freezing. Come on."

He still wore his suit and the dress coat from the party. At least she could bulk up in warm layers. No way was he not freezing out here.

"Wait a second." His eyes searched the ground near her house. Slowly, he took a step, then another. "Go on inside if you don't want to wait, but I heard a cat."

A cat? She didn't own a cat. Compassion was not in her genetic makeup, so she'd spared all animals and sworn to never own one. She wouldn't have the first clue what to do if left in charge of a living, breathing thing.

Just as she reached for the door handle, Braden crouched down. Zara gasped when he pulled a snow-covered kitten up in his gloved hands. Instantly he cradled the animal to his chest and swiped the snow off its back.

Braden took cautious steps toward the back door, keeping the kitten tucked firmly just inside his coat. Zara realized his intentions immediately.

"You're bringing that inside?"

His eyes went from the gray bundle to her. "Yes. He'll freeze to death out here. He's wet and shivering."

Zara glanced around. "Where's the mom? Aren't animals made to live outside? They have fur on."

His brows shot up. "You have a coat on, too. Do you want to stay out here and see if you survive?"

Swallowing, she shook her head. "Um…so what do we do once it's inside?"

Braden tipped his head to the side. "You've never had a pet, have you?"

"Never."

Braden's sharp gaze softened. "Let's talk inside. This little guy needs warmth, and so do we."

Zara opened the back door and ushered Braden in ahead of her. Once they had their coats and boots off, Braden started searching her cabinets. He seemed to be satisfied with the box of crackers he'd found.

"Grab a bowl of water and let's get back upstairs where it's warm."

Without waiting on her, he took the box and the kitten and disappeared. Okay, so he'd basically ordered her around in her own home and that was after bringing in a stray animal.

Was badass Braden O'Shea brought to his knees over a little bundle of fur? Zara nearly laughed as she pulled out a shallow bowl and filled it with water. By the time she got upstairs, Braden was sitting on the edge of the bed, the kitten at his side, as he peeled off his socks. His feet were red and had to be absolutely freezing.

"These got soaked," he told her. "The snow went right into my boots."

"Let me have those." Placing the water on the floor at the foot of the bed, Zara reached out and took the soaked, icy socks.

"My pants are wet, too."

Her eyes darted up to his. That smirk on his face had her shaking her head. "Oh, no. Don't even think of stripping. You can roll the pant legs up and come sit by the fire."

His big hand stroked over the cat as the damp animal snuggled deeper into her cream duvet. "You're no fun at all."

"Oh, I'm loads of fun. I'm an events coordinator. I get paid to be fun."

After she laid his socks by the gas logs, which she cranked

up because she was still shivering, she turned back to see Braden feeding the kitten small bites of a cracker. For a second she just stood there and stared. She'd not met many men like Braden, hard and powerful on one hand, soft and compassionate on the other.

"You're staring," he stated without looking up.

She remained where she was because the sight of him on her bed being so…adorable was not something she'd planned on. She'd had a hard enough time resisting him when he'd been flat-out sexy. Now that an adorable factor had slipped right in, she was losing what little control she had left.

How would she handle another night with this man?

Six

So now Zara was not only nervous around him, she was nervous over a cat. This woman had so many complex layers, and damn if he didn't want to peel back each one.

"I'm going to take my pants off if you keep looking at me like that," he threatened. He didn't know what was going through her mind, but he couldn't handle her looking at him as if he was some savior or something.

"I'm just trying to figure you out."

His hand stilled on the kitten's boney back. "Don't," he told her, meeting her gaze across the room. "That's not an area you want to go to."

Zara crossed to the chaise and shoved her blanket aside before taking a seat and curling her feet beneath her. "Oh, I think maybe I do want to go there. What makes a rumored bad boy go all soft with a kitten?"

"I wouldn't have left any animal out in this. Would you?"

He needed to turn the topic of conversation back to her. Nothing good would come from her digging into his private life, but he wanted to know more and more about hers. Suddenly, finding out more intimate details had less to do with the scrolls…not that finding those weren't still his top priority.

"Honestly, if I'd been alone, I wouldn't have known what to do. I guess maybe I would've brought it in, but I seriously thought animals were made to be outside."

Braden reached into the sleeve of crackers for another and broke off a piece for the kitten. "Why no pets growing up?"

He watched from the corner of his eye as she toyed with the edge of her sweatshirt a moment before speaking. She was either nervous or contemplating how much to tell— most likely a little of both. Fine by him. He would wait.

"My parents weren't the most affectionate," she started slowly, as if finding the right way to describe her mom and dad was difficult. "To be honest, I never asked for a pet. I figured they'd say no, so I didn't bother."

When the kitten turned away and stretched before nestling deeper into the covers, Braden set the crackers on the nightstand before shifting on the bed to face her.

"Were they affectionate to you?" he asked, wondering why he was allowing himself this line of questioning. Seduction was one thing, but finding out about her childhood was a whole other level he didn't need to get into in order to do the job he came to do.

"It doesn't matter."

Suddenly it did. Braden came to his feet and padded over to join her on the narrow chaise. Easing a knee up on to the cushion, he turned sideways.

"Were you abused?" he asked, almost afraid of the answer. "Is that why you had such a strong connection with your grandmother?"

"Oh, no." Zara shook her head. "I wasn't abused. There were and are kids who have worse lives. I guess I've just always felt sorry for myself because of all the things I think I missed out on. But, they gave me a nice house, toys, camps in the summer."

"Family vacations?" he asked.

"Um…no. They went on trips and cruises while I was away at camp. When they traveled during the school year, I would stay with my grandmother." A sad smile spread across her face. "To be honest, those were the best times of my childhood. I loved spending time here. Gram would make up a scavenger hunt, and I'd spend hours exploring all these old rooms and hideout areas."

"Hideouts?" he asked. Damn, he felt like a jerk for listening to her, caring what she was actually saying and now turning it around to benefit his plan. Still, the end result would be the same. He would find those scrolls, and Zara was going to have to inadvertently help. "I know my house is old and has secret areas. I assume this one does, too?"

Zara smiled and tipped her head to meet his gaze. "Yeah. There's a hidden door beneath the stairs. It actually takes you into the den at the back of the house. In the basement there's a couple of hidden rooms, but they're so narrow, they're more like closets."

He wanted to check those areas out right this second, but he had to remain motionless and let her continue. Once she was asleep he'd be able to continue his quest. Those secret rooms she'd mentioned weren't on the blueprints he'd seen, and his father had never mentioned them, so he had to assume no one had checked there, either.

"My grandmother always told me how much she loved me," Zara went on, her voice almost a whisper as if she were talking to herself. "She always told me how I was her biggest treasure. I didn't get that until recently. I look at all the antiques in this old house, pieces I know are worth a lot of money. But to know she valued me even more…"

Braden continued to watch her battle her emotions, trying to remain strong and hold back. He admired her strength, her dignity and pride.

Slowly, Braden was sinking into her world—a world he never intended to be a part of. If he could somehow get away with taking back the scrolls, maybe they could see where this attraction led.

Damn it. All this secret snooping was supposed to be Ryker's area. Braden and Mac were more the powerhouse guys who ran everything smoothly and kept a few cops and federal agents on their payroll to keep their reputation clean.

"I'm sorry." Zara let out a soft laugh. "I didn't mean to get all nostalgic and sentimental on you."

Braden reached out, placing a hand on her knee. Her body stilled beneath his as her eyes widened. "Don't apologize for talking to me. We're more than employee/employer at this point."

Zara's actions betrayed her as her gaze darted to his mouth, then back up. She may have been stiff beneath his touch, but she couldn't hold back her emotions. Those striking eyes gave everything away.

She pulled in a deep breath. "What happened last night—"

"Wasn't nearly enough," he finished. "The pace we set is up to you, but the end result is inevitable."

Zara shifted her knee and turned to face him, mirroring him. His hand fell away, but he stretched his arm along the back of the chaise as he waited for her to offer up some excuse as to why they shouldn't explore this chemistry.

"I need this job."

He smiled. "And you were the best candidate, that's why I hired you." *Well, one of the reasons.* "Your job has nothing to do with what's going on between us."

"Nothing is going on," she all but yelled, throwing her arms wide. "Nothing can go on. Not while I'm working for you."

Braden shrugged. "Fine. You're fired."

Zara tipped her head, glaring at him from beneath heavy lids. "That's ridiculous."

"I always get what I want, Zara."

"And you're that desperate for a bedmate?"

Leaning forward, his fingertips found the side of her face, stroking down to her neck where she trembled. "No. Just you."

"Why?" she whispered.

"Why not?" he retorted.

The pulse beneath his hand jumped as he leaned in a bit closer. Her warm breath tickled him, the flare in her eyes motivated him and her parted lips begged him.

His other hand came up to cup the side of her face. His thumb stroked over her full bottom lip. Never once did she take her eyes off his, and while the power appeared to be completely his right now, this woman, who had him in unexpected knots, could flip that role at any moment and bring him to his knees. And the fact that she had no clue about her control over him made her even sexier.

He continued to stroke her lip as his other hand slid around to cup the back of her head. His fingers threaded through her hair, massaging as he went. A soft sigh escaped her, and Braden's entire body tightened in response.

"You're not thinking work right now, are you?" he whispered against her lips. "You're concentrating on my touch, on how you want more."

"What are you doing to me?" she asked as her lids lowered.

"Proving a point."

Her tongue darted out to lick her lips, brushing against his thumb, instantly flipping that control. His completely snapped with that simple move.

Braden captured her mouth beneath his, not caring for finesse or gentleness. There was only so much a man could handle. Zara's hands came up and fisted the front of his shirt as she moaned...music to his ears.

Tipping his head slightly, Braden changed the angle of the kiss. When Zara leaned into him, he wanted to drag her into his lap and speed this process along. So he did.

Gripping her around the waist, without breaking the kiss, Braden shifted to sit forward as he placed her over his lap.

Instantly her legs straddled his thighs, and her hands slid up over his shoulders as the heated kiss continued. Braden hadn't wanted a woman this bad in a long time…maybe never. Zara was sexy, yes, but there was more to her than anything superficial, and he wanted more. He wanted all she would give.

His hands slid beneath the hem of her sweatshirt. That smooth skin beneath his palms could make any man beg. He was near that point. Who knew he'd actually find a weakness in his life? He prided himself on being strong, being in control.

Just as his thumbs brushed the silk on her bra, Zara jerked back, pushing against his shoulders.

"Wait," she gasped. "We—we can't do this."

Scrambling off his lap, she held her fingers to her lips and closed her eyes. Was she trying to keep that sensation a while longer? Was she still tasting him? Braden waited. She was seriously battling with herself.

"Kissing me like that…" Zara sighed, dropped her arms and looked him in the eyes. "I can't want this, Braden. Don't you understand?"

Relaxed against the back cushion, Braden eyed her, letting her stand above him, giving her the upper hand here. A smart businessman knew when to pull back on the reins in order to get ahead.

"Why are you denying yourself?" he asked. "If the job wasn't a factor, what other excuse would you use?"

He'd hit a mark. Her chin when up a notch, her eyes narrowed. "I'm not making excuses. Nothing would've happened between us at all had you not been stuck here. The next time I would've seen you would've been at the party you're throwing in five weeks for all of your employees."

Braden laughed, shaking his head.

"Now you're laughing at me?" she asked, crossing her arms.

Slowly coming to his feet, Braden crossed to her, not a

bit surprised when she didn't back up, but tipped her head back to continue to glare.

"I'm laughing at the fact you think we wouldn't have seen each other." He tucked a portion of her hair behind her ear, purposely trailing his fingertips down her cheek. "Zara, I would've found reasons to see you. The fact I'm stuck here only provided me the opportunity I needed to seduce you properly."

Silence settled between them seconds before Zara moaned and threw her arms out to her sides as she spun toward the logs and went to stand before them. "Your ego is something I hadn't taken into account. Maybe you've forgotten I just ended a relationship with a man who thought he could control me, thought he was in charge."

Braden stared at her back, deciding to let that jab about Shane roll off him. He knew he wasn't anything like that bastard. She knew it, too.

"I didn't say I wanted a relationship," he corrected. "And I know you well enough after hearing about your childhood to say you don't, either."

Zara whirled around, her dark hair flying about her shoulders. "You think you know me? Because I gave you a small portion of my life?"

"So you do want a relationship?"

"Stop twisting my words."

Why was he purposely getting under her skin? This wasn't part of his plan, but seeing Zara worked up and verbally sparring with her was more of a turn-on than he'd thought. He needed to steer things back to where she felt in control, where she felt as if he was less of a threat. He knew she wanted him, she knew it, too, stubborn woman. But for now he'd let this moment pass. The ultimate goal was still pressing, and he had work to do.

"Why don't you show me those secret rooms?" he asked, pleased when her eyes widened.

"What?"

"Those rooms. They sound cool, and I'd like to see them."

Her eyes darted to the kitten, still sleeping on the bed. "What about him?"

Braden walked over, scooped the kitten into his arm and motioned toward the door. "All set."

"It's cold in the rest of the house."

He quirked a brow. "You want to stay in here and keep dancing around the sexual tension?"

She moved to the door so fast, Braden couldn't stop laughing. Finally he was getting somewhere. He may not be getting her into his bed, but he was seeing these illusive rooms and perhaps he'd find something, anything, to hint at the scrolls. When all was said and done, and this freak blizzard was over, he'd have all his wishes fulfilled.

Seven

Zara gripped the neck of her sweatshirt as she came down the wide staircase. Trying to hold it up just a bit more to ward off the chill helped.

Eerie quiet settled throughout the house. Who knew darkness had a tone? She could hear Braden's breathing, his every step, every brush of his clothing. Every single thing he did made her even more aware of his presence.

What the hell had she been thinking kissing him back like that? Straddling his lap and practically crawling all over his body? Part of her was mortified she'd acted like that, but on the other hand, he'd been right there with her. He'd been the one to instigate every heated occurrence. But no more. If he touched her, she'd have to walk away. Even if she had to step out into the cold hall or bundle up and sleep in a chilly spare bedroom, she couldn't let him kiss her again.

Because she feared the next kiss would lead to clothes falling off and them tumbling into bed.

With the mid-morning sun shining in the windows, enough

light filtered through to make this encounter not seem so intimate.

She led him to the den and eased the door open. "This room was never used by my grandmother. She usually just put books in here. I think I'm the only one who ever came in here, and that was just because I wanted to get to the secret passageway. As a kid, that was the coolest thing in the world to me."

"Did you ever have friends over?" he asked as he stepped into the room with her. "This house would've made the greatest backdrop for hide-and-seek."

"I had a few friends sleep over," she admitted. "Looking back now, I only brought friends here. My parents wouldn't have gone for me inviting them to our house. They were always going to some party, throwing a party or worried about their next travel venture."

Braden loathed her parents. Why bring a child into this world if you didn't intend on caring for said child? He admitted he wanted kids, when the time was right. Having them now would be ridiculous because he didn't have the time to devote to them. And children needed structure, needed family and a bond that provided security.

Zara was a strong woman, but he could see the vulnerability, the brokenness of her childhood still affecting her today.

Stepping around him, she pulled the flashlight from beneath her arm. "Follow me."

One of the built-in bookcases had a small latch. Zara jerked once, twice, and finally the hinges creaked open. As she flicked on the light and angled the beam into the darkness, Braden's heart kicked up. He desperately wanted to find what he came for, though realistically he figured things wouldn't be that easy.

The kitten purred against Braden's chest. He'd never owned a cat, but he loved animals. His sister would be so happy to take in another stray. She was the proverbial cat lady, though she'd never own up to the term. Laney would take this kitten in with a squeal of delight. He could already envision her snuggling the thing.

Braden stepped into the narrow hallway behind Zara. "Don't worry if that door closes behind you. We can't get trapped in here. I guess whoever owned this before my grandmother had a latch installed on both ends of the tunnel. My guess is someone got locked in, so they learned their lesson."

Locked in a dark place with Zara…not too far off the mark of how they'd spent last night. And not a bad predicament to be in.

The kitten perked up at Zara's voice and leaped out of Braden's arms. The little thing moved so fast, Braden worried he'd hurt himself, but when the kitten slid against Zara's ankles, he figured the animal was just fine.

Zara's flashlight held steady on the stray. "What is he doing?"

With a laugh, Braden continued to watch the cat seeking affection. "Looks like he wants to be friends."

"I have enough friends," she muttered and tried to take a step. When she tripped over the kitten, Braden held out a hand to steady her. "Will she stop trying to be an ankle bracelet anytime soon?"

"If you pick her up," Braden stated. "Cats have a tendency to cling to one person. You may be the chosen one."

With the light casting enough of a glow, Braden saw her eyes widen. "You're kidding."

"Nope."

Reluctantly, Zara plucked up the kitten, held her in a bit of an awkward way, but the little fur ball didn't seem to mind. Braden felt it best not to mention the obvious that the cat seemed to love Zara. Best move on to the point of this tour.

"Is this just a hallway?" he asked, trying to look on the

walls for any compartments or doors…hell, anything that would be a clue as to where he could search.

"It opens up into a little room before letting you out into the kitchen."

Zara let out a grunt, the flashlight bobbed and Braden used his free arm to reach out as she tumbled forward. His arm banded around her waist, his hand connected with her breast as he supported her from falling. Thankfully the kitten was snuggled tight, and Zara had a good grip on the oblivious little thing.

When Zara fell back against him, he didn't relinquish his hold. How could he when she felt too perfect with her body flush against his?

"Thanks," she whispered. "I forgot there's a bit of a dip in the floor right there."

"Are you all right?" he asked.

She nodded, her hair tickling the side of his face. "Um… you can let me go."

Her body arched, betraying her words. He couldn't stop himself. His thumb slid back and forth across her breast before he reluctantly released her. He wanted her aching for him, for his touch. If he kept pushing, she'd completely close off, and he'd look like more of a jerk that what he was. But keeping her body on high alert, having her wonder about what would happen next between them would inevitably have her in his bed. Well, technically her bed.

She said nothing as she continued on, slower this time. Finally they came to the room she'd mentioned, which wasn't more than a walk-in closet in size. Her light darted around, and she gasped. His eyes followed the beam and landed on a little yellow chair; a book lay open, cover up to hold the page. Zara turned and handed him the kitten.

"I used to sneak in here to read." She moved forward and picked up the book, flipping it over in her hand. With a laugh, she laid it back down. "This was one of my favorites."

Braden crossed the space and glanced down to the book.

He couldn't see the title, but the embracing couple on the cover told him all he needed to know.

"You read romance as a kid?"

"I was a teenager and curious," she said. Even in the dim light he could see her chin pop up a notch. "Maybe I wanted to know what all that love stuff was about, because when I was sixteen I thought I'd found love. Turns out I found a guy who'd made a bet with his buddies on who would take my virginity."

That entire statement told him more about her than she'd ever willingly reveal. She was bitter, she'd been used. She was raised by parents who were never affectionate, and other than her grandmother, she didn't have anyone she could depend on in her life.

Coming from a large Irish family, Braden had no clue what that felt like. Granted he'd never fallen in love, but he believed it existed. He'd witnessed it firsthand from his parents. While he'd had so many levels of love, Zara had emptiness.

"So you would sneak in here and read dirty books?" he asked.

"They weren't dirty. They were sweet, and now that I know how life really is, I see why they're labeled as fiction."

Yeah. Definitely bitter.

He scanned the rest of the area. There were a few empty shelves along one wall, a door on the other and absolutely nothing of use for him in here. Except for the bundles of information he'd just gathered on Zara.

"That concludes the tour," she stated. "Not as exciting as you thought, right?"

Braden shifted the kitten to his other arm, careful not to wake him. "Oh, I wouldn't say that. I got to cop a feel. I wouldn't call this venture a total loss."

For a second she said nothing, then she reached out and smacked his shoulder. "You're a smart-ass."

Braden wanted to see that smile she offered. He craved

it. Knowing he pulled her from those past thoughts with his snarky comment and put her in the here and now with a laugh was exactly his intent.

"Why don't you show me the other hidden rooms, and I'll see what other smooth moves I can come up with?" he suggested, which earned him a light right to the face. Squinting, he shielded his eyes with his free hand. "All right, I promise to be on my best behavior."

Turning away, Zara pushed open the door to the kitchen. "You'll have to do better than that," she muttered.

Nothing. He'd not found a damn thing that indicated where the scrolls were. He didn't even know if they were all together at this point. At one time there were nine, stored in the infamous trunk that now sat in his office as if to mock him on a daily basis. They could be long gone, but Braden refused to give into that line of thinking, because if they were gone, he had absolutely nowhere to look. They had to be here.

Before they'd headed back up to the bedroom, Zara had stepped out the back door and plucked some cheese and fruit out of the snow. She pulled a loaf of bread from the cabinet and got a few bottles of water.

Now they were sitting in the floor in front of the fire having a gourmet lunch while the kitten roamed around the room. Occasionally he would come back, rub against Zara as if to make sure she was still there, then he'd roam a little more.

"Is he going to pee on my things?" she asked, popping a grape into her mouth.

Braden shrugged. "Maybe, but I found a box in your kitchen and brought it up. Put a towel or something over there and he'll be very happy. Cats love boxes."

"Really?"

Nodding, he tore off another hunk of cheese. "Trust me on this. Granted, he's still a kitten, so he'll stick close to us, or you as the case may be, but once he gets comfortable here, that box will be his new home."

Zara stared as the kitten snuck beneath her bed. "I'd rather he find a new home."

"Aww, now don't be like that with your new best friend."

By the time they'd devoured the assortment, Zara leaned back and stretched her arms high above her head, pulling her sweatshirt up just enough to draw his gaze down to her creamy skin and the slight roll over the band of her pants.

"I wish the electricity would come back on," she stated, dropping her arms, oblivious to the knots in his gut. "I have so much work to do. My laptop may only have a couple hours left of charge."

"What are you working on?"

"I have an event scheduled for a client in four weeks. I need to adjust some things on the spreadsheets and set up another schedule for an event I'm working on for a bridal party." Zara started picking up the garbage and bundling it all in the empty bread sack. "Plenty of work to do with no Wi-Fi, but I'm going to get backed up if I can't get some emails done in the next few days."

Braden listened to her talk of the event scheduled a week before his next party. Zara was efficient, and the passion for her work came through in her tone. She definitely was career driven, but was that all there was to her life? He'd not heard her mention friends and he knew there was no boyfriend. He'd never met a woman who remained so closed off on a personal level.

"Why don't you work?" he suggested. "I'm going to head to my car, charge my phone and turn it on to make some calls."

He needed to check in with Ryker to see if he'd located the missing art piece in London. Then he needed to see if Mac was stuck at the main house, most likely since Mac's flight back to Miami would've been canceled with this weather. Braden would have to call his sister, too, because…

well, he worried about her even though she hated her older brothers fussing over her.

Hopping to her feet, Zara nodded. "Yeah. I need to do something. I'm not one to sit still and do nothing. After I draft my emails I'm grabbing a shower."

"With cold water?" he asked.

She smiled down at him. "I have a gas hot water heater."

His eyes raked over her body, and the very last thing he needed was an image of her naked, soapy and wet body with only a thin door separating them.

Rising to stand before her, he took the trash from her hands and headed for the bedroom door. "I'll be in my car for a while. I'll throw this away on my way out."

He left the room before he would give into temptation and join her in the shower. He needed to let Mac know that, so far, nothing had turned up. This house was damn big, but the secret hidey-holes were literally bare, save for the yellow chair and romance novel.

After throwing away the trash and bundling up, Braden tried to get through the mounds of snow to his car. There was no way to get there without soaking his feet once again because the snow was up to his knees; but he needed to check in, and once the engine warmed up, he could put the heater on full blast.

Most likely his battery would've been fine to talk inside the warm house, but he couldn't risk Zara overhearing his conversations.

Powering up his phone as he slid behind the wheel and tried to ignore his freezing wet feet, Braden watched as seven texts popped up on his screen. Mac had sent two, and the other five were from a frantic Laney asking if he was all right.

He decided to call her first because an angry woman, especially an angry Irish woman who happened to be his sister, was not someone he wanted on his bad side.

"You better be in a ditch with little cell service," she answered.

Braden laughed. "Not quite in a ditch, but I'm stuck at a friend's house and the electricity is out."

"What friend?" she asked, skepticism dripping from her voice.

"You don't know her."

"Her? So you're shacking up and can't return my texts? I had you lying in a ditch bleeding and with the roads closed, and no one saw you and you'd died all alone."

Braden pinched the bridge of his nose and sighed. "I assure you, I'm fine, and I'm not shacking up. To be honest, I'd feel better if I was."

Laney laughed. "Whoever she is, I want to meet her. Someone has you in knots. I like her already."

He wasn't in knots. Really, he was completely knot free and in total control. Just because he'd had to physically remove himself from the house since Zara was going to shower didn't mean he couldn't keep his wits about him.

"I'm at Zara's, okay?" He tried to keep his tone level so she didn't read any more into what he was saying. "I was worried about the roads, so I offered her a ride home. On the way, I got pulled over by a deputy and was informed there's a level two snow emergency on the roads and I was to stay put. So here I am."

"Aww, poor baby. Stuck in a house with a beautiful woman. Don't think I didn't see you two dancing at the party. And great job getting into the house, by the way. If I didn't know better, I'd think you had some weather god on your payroll, as well."

"Yeah, I've turned up nothing. But I'm not done yet. I'm hoping to loosen Zara up enough to get her talking. She may not even realize she knows something useful."

"You sound crankier than usual," Laney mocked. "No scrolls, no sex. I hope you're not acting like a bear toward your hostess."

Cranking the heat up, Braden dropped his head back against the seat. "Now that you know I'm alive and sexually frustrated, can we be done with this call?"

Laney laughed even harder. "Only because I love you am I letting you off the hook. Don't think I won't be discussing this with Mac."

"I've no doubt you'll do so as soon as we hang up," he muttered. "Are you okay? You're home?"

"I'm fine. Carter stayed over last night, which was a good thing because I couldn't get my generator started."

Well, at least Carter was good for one thing, but Braden still considered Laney's boyfriend a prick.

Braden bit his tongue, because if Carter kept treating his sister as if she should be thanking him for a relationship, Braden was going to step in. He'd seen too many times how Carter would act as if he was doing Laney a favor by being with her. He'd even hinted once that she'd be lonely without him. No way in hell would Delaney O'Shea be lonely. She was gorgeous, she was successful and she was a member of the most powerful family in Boston. They were never alone.

He said his goodbyes before he said something that would drive a wedge between them. He'd much rather deal with Carter on his own terms. But, at least the guy had been there during the storm, and his sister was safe. Braden would keep that in mind when he actually confronted him…and that day was coming sooner rather than later.

Braden turned the heat down, now that he was thawed out and his feet weren't so chilled. He quickly dialed Mac, only to get his voice mail.

"Hey, man. I'm stuck at Zara's house, little cell service. I'll call back when I can, but nothing has been found yet."

He disconnected the call and stared back at the house. He wondered just how long he'd have to sit out here to avoid seeing her glowing, damp body from the shower all under the pretense of letting his phone charge. He had plenty of charge to go back in, but he figured he'd let it fill up.

He needed to keep a little distance from her because he was having a hard enough time controlling this ache. He didn't like the unfamiliar need that seemed to grow stronger with each passing moment.

No need in going back in just yet, because he knew without a doubt that once he saw Zara partially nude again, there would be nothing holding him back.

Eight

Feeling refreshed after her shower, Zara found another pair of sweats and fuzzy socks. More armor to fight off the sexy man with seduction on the brain.

Okay, fine. Sex was on her mind, too, but she couldn't let herself settle too far into that part of her brain because, honestly, the sex she'd had with guys in the past had just been…meh. And she wasn't about to risk her job on some mediocre moment. Besides, if they had sex now, what if he was stuck here for two more days? Seriously. Talk about a new level of awkward. Added to that, would he expect a replay? Was he a one-and-done man?

Zara groaned as she took out her frustrations by towel-drying her hair. Why was she overanalyzing this? She wasn't shedding her fleece, no matter what tricky moves he put on her.

Zara hung her towel on the knob of her closet door. No way was she going back out to the bathroom. While the water had been nice and hot, the room itself was an icebox. There was no master bath in this house, but the bathroom was right outside her bedroom door. Still, given she was damp and her hair was still drying, that would make for one cold walk.

Grabbing her brush from the dresser, she took a seat on her bed and crossed her legs as she pulled her hair over her shoulder and started working out the tangles at the bottom.

That kitten darted out from beneath her bed, and Zara just knew that thing was making a litter box out of the space. Once again the bundle of fur slid against Zara's ankles and feet, purring as he went. Even though she'd never had an animal, she honestly didn't mind that it was in her house. She may not have a clue how to care for a pet, but she didn't want the thing outside freezing to death. Okay, and maybe she kind of liked knowing something was looking to her for care and support. She didn't necessarily love it, but she had a kernel of like.

The bedroom door opened as Braden came sliding back in. Immediately he went to the fire and peeled off his wet socks once again. Zara sighed, tapping the brush against her thigh.

"Why don't you go hop in the shower and warm up your feet? And when you're done, I'll give you a pair of my socks. They're small, but they're warm and dry." When he didn't say anything, he merely turned and stared at her, she went on. "Maybe stop going outside. Whatever you need, I can go. I at least have taller boots."

Raking a hand through his hair, Braden strode back out the door. Apparently he was taking her up on the shower. But what had happened in the time he'd walked out until now? He seemed quiet, wouldn't quite look her in the eyes. Something was wrong.

The O'Sheas were mysterious and closed off, so she'd never know. But she didn't want him upset or angry. It was freezing, they were stuck. Oh, yeah, and sexually frustrated. That made for a nice combo.

While he was gone, Zara got an idea and snuck out to the kitchen. Finding exactly what she needed, she raced back up to the bedroom. The shower was still running, so she had time to set up. Apparently he'd found towels and was making himself at home. Granted, all she had were floral specialty soaps, but she'd not exactly prepared for male guests.

Zara moved the chaise back closer to the wall to open up the middle of the floor. She settled down, crossing her legs and had the necessary items in front of her just as Braden came back in...wearing only a towel.

"You've got to be kidding me," she muttered.

Without a word, he crossed the room and laid his clothes out in front of the fire. "Unlike you, I don't have the luxury of throwing on different clothes. I've been wearing these since yesterday morning."

She glanced over and seriously wished she hadn't. Were those...yeah. He was a black boxer brief man. No tighty-whities for this alpha male...and seeing his underwear made it crystal clear he was commando beneath that terry cloth.

Braden cleared his throat, and she realized he'd turned and was staring at her. Great. Way to really hold her ground about not getting intimate when she's caught staring at the man's underwear.

"What's this?" he asked, motioning down to her stash.

She ignored the items she'd brought up from the kitchen and continued to stare up at him as if having a conversation wearing only a towel were perfectly normal.

"So you're going to be like this until your clothes dry?" She motioned with her finger up and down his body.

Clutching one side of the towel over one very muscular, very exposed thigh, Braden shrugged. "I can lose the towel, but I thought you'd be more comfortable like this."

Zara rolled her eyes. The man was proving to be impossible to resist, and she truly didn't know how much longer she could hold out.

"I'm comfortable with your clothes on," she muttered. "Anyway, I thought we could play cards, and since I'm not one to gamble, I brought up pretzel sticks we can use instead."

He quirked a brow. "You play poker?"

Zara laughed. "You didn't know my grandmother. That woman could outwit the best of the best when it came to seven-card stud. She taught me how to play when I was still learning how to write my name."

Braden quirked his brow, then headed over to the chaise and pulled off the blanket she used to sleep with. He wrapped it around his waist and sank to the floor in front of her.

That bare chest with dark hair and just a bit of ink showing over his shoulder held her captive, and she would have to concentrate on this game if she wanted to control her urge to rip that blanket and towel from his deliciously sculpted body.

"Can you play?" she asked, pulling the cards from the box.

Piercing eyes held hers. "I can play whatever game you want."

Of course he could, and he could make everything sound sexual with that low, intense tone that had her stomach doing flips.

When she offered the cards to him to shuffle, he waved a hand. "Ladies first."

Shuffling them with quick, precise movements, Zara finally felt comfortable. Cards was something she could handle, something she could somewhat control. A hobby of hers from long ago, she hadn't played for a while, but she needed the distraction, and there was only so much they could do stuck in this room.

"What's the ante?" he asked, tearing open the bag of pretzels.

"Your choice."

"Ten."

Zara dealt their first hand while he counted out twenty pretzel sticks for each of them. As soon as she laid down the door card, she smiled when his was lower than hers.

"Your bet," she told him.

He smirked. "I'm aware of the rules."

"Just making sure you know you're dealing with a professional."

There. Maybe if she kept throwing verbiage out like that, he wouldn't be so determined to cross territory they could never return from.

Braden raised the bet, but Zara didn't think he had anything worth raising for. She'd call him on his bluff. He had a poker face, that was for sure. No doubt he'd used that same straight, stoic look in the business world. As the oldest son of the late Patrick O'Shea, Braden had big shoes to fill, and being the powerful man he was, he'd have no problem at all, Zara knew.

By the time the last card was dealt, Zara was looking at a full house with aces on top. Not the best hand, but still better than whatever he was lying about.

"I'll raise you," she told him, throwing in three more sticks.

When he flipped his cards over, Zara gripped her cards and simply stared. Seriously? She'd dealt him a flush? There hadn't been a gleam in his eye one time during the entire game, and she'd thought he'd been bluffing.

Narrowing her eyes, she tossed her cards down as he raked in his pretzels. The kitten chose that time to dart over and walk right through the cards and the pretzels as if he owned the place. He swatted at a pretzel and kept swatting it until he was moving too close to the logs. There was a screen around the fireplace, more for looks, but she still didn't want the little guy rubbing against it and singeing his fur.

Zara reached out, stretching to grab hold of him and his

pretzel, then deposited him on the other side of her away from the heat.

"I believe it's my deal," Braden stated with a smirk. "Hold tight. We're about to take this to a whole new level."

She tipped her head in a silent question.

"We're playing for answers now," he told her as he reached down, grabbed a pretzel and popped it into his mouth. "Whoever wins the hand can ask the other player anything, and they have to answer."

Still eyeing him skeptically, Zara asked, "Just questions? No touching, no clichéd strip poker?"

Shuffling the cards, he smiled. "I'll touch and strip if you want. Hell, that can even be one of your questions. Up to you, so ask what you want."

Mercy, the man was incorrigible, and she was finding that she loved every second of his quick wit, his flirty side and the fact he made no secret that he wanted her.

Thankfully, she won the next hand with a pair of kings, beating out his jacks. Zara reached to push the cards back in order to shuffle them as she pondered her question.

Staring down at the cards as they shuffled and fell into place, she asked, "If you believe in marriage and family so much, why are you still single?"

That sexy laugh filled the room. "I'm so glad you didn't ask something as boring as my favorite color or movie."

Risking a glance, she looked him in the eye. Okay, fine, her eyes may have lingered a little longer on his bare chest, but they eventually hit his eyes, where she saw amusement staring back at her.

"Well?" she asked, raising her brows as she started dealing.

"Haven't found the right one."

He studied his cards, offering nothing else with his response. Zara gritted her teeth. If he was going to be vague, then so could she when the time came…though she didn't intend to lose.

As she stared at her cards, though, a pit grew in her stomach. Unless she was dealt something spectacular in the next round, she was going to be answering a question, and she was almost afraid to see what he'd come up with.

The second he realized he won, he dropped a question she definitely hadn't expected.

"Why do you choose assholes to date? Because of commitment issues?"

Zara refused to be rattled. "That's two questions, so your round is disqualified."

Just as she reached for the cards, Braden's hand covered hers. As if knowing he was naked beneath that blanket weren't enough to sizzle her mind, his warm touch only added fuel to the proverbial fire.

"I'm not disqualified." Gently squeezing her hand, he turned her palm over and laced their fingers, holding their joined hands up between them. "Tell me why you only date jerks."

"How do you know I date jerks?"

His thumb stroked hers as he spoke, as if the man were trying to put her under a spell. Too late. He'd done that the moment she'd walked into his office months ago. But once he'd held her at the party, once he'd shown a more personal side, she'd turned a corner and she wasn't sure she could ever get back.

"Who did you date before Shane?" he asked.

Zara stared at him for a second before laughing. Damn. That came out sounding nervous. She wasn't nervous. Just because he was holding her hand, looking at her as if he cared and asking about her love life. Why should any of that worry her?

And even as much as all of that worried her, it was the desire, the lust staring back at her that had her stomach in knots.

"You're asking way too many questions," she whispered.

"Your silence tells me all I need to know." Inching closer,

he set the cards between them and kept his eyes locked on to hers. "You don't like commitment because your parents weren't loving or affectionate. You didn't get the attention a child deserves. Now as an adult you're dating jerks because you know you won't get attached. Same reason you haven't unpacked, if I'm guessing right. You can't even commit to this house."

Zara jerked her hand back. "Whatever you're trying to prove, stop. You don't know me well enough to analyze me."

Coming to her feet, she smoothed her hair back from her face. "I'm done playing."

Before she could turn away, Braden slowly rose. That predator look in his eyes as he closed the space between them held her firmly in place. The fact he could be so menacing, so arousing while holding on to a bulky comforter at his waist with one hand proved just how far she'd fallen from her initial mind-set. She was crumbling right at this man's feet.

And the more her resolve deteriorated, the more she wondered, why was she holding back? He'd pegged her perfectly when he said she wasn't looking for any commitment. First, she didn't have time with her business soaking up her life. Second, well, she just didn't want to. She wouldn't have any idea how. Since she'd signed on with the O'Sheas, she'd seen the close-knit family they were. A piece of her wondered what a connection that strong would be like. Leaning on someone else, expecting support was too much of a risk. But she didn't need a man.

He'd made it clear he didn't want a commitment, though. Once the roads cleared he'd be gone, and whatever happened here would stay right here. Braden wasn't one to talk, of that she was sure. Her reputation wouldn't be tarnished, she wouldn't be known as the woman who slept with her clients or her boss. Honestly, what was holding her back?

From the look in Braden's eyes, he wasn't looking for a walk down the aisle...just a walk to the bed.

Nine

Braden didn't know what changed, but the look of determination and stubbornness was wiped clean. Now Zara stared back at him with passion blazing in those striking eyes. She didn't step forward to meet him, but she no longer looked as if she wanted to flee the room.

As he stood within touching distance, Braden took in the rapid pulse at the base of her throat, her shallow breathing and wide eyes. She wasn't thinking how angry she was now.

"You're not running," he muttered, delighting in the fact she tipped her head up to look at him instead of backing up. Braden reached out, tucking her hair behind her ear and sliding his fingertip along her jawline. "Why is that, Zara?"

"Because this is my house, and I'm not afraid of you."

For such a petite woman, he was impressed. He intimidated men twice her size, yet this woman wasn't backing down. He admired her—more than he should, because all he wanted from her on a personal level was right here and right now. The scroll business had no place in this bedroom.

"Or maybe you're finally giving in," he stated, raking his finger over her bottom lip. "Maybe you see that we're both adults, we're stuck here together and this attraction isn't going away."

Her chin tipped up a notch. "Maybe I am."

Braden smiled at her bold statement. How could he not find her charming and sexy and confident all rolled into one perfect package?

Wait. Perfect? No. Nobody was perfect, but she was perfect for him right at this moment.

In all of his thirty-five years, Braden had been taught to take chances to get what he wanted. There was no greater time to test that theory than right now.

Braden dropped the comforter and the towel. Both fell to his feet without a sound. The light coming through the plantation shutters gave enough for her to see that he was completely ready for her.

"You have all the control now," he told her. "Whatever you want to do from this point on is your call. You can humiliate me and reject me, you can quit your job and claim I'm just like the jerks you dated, or you can start stripping out of those clothes and join me by the fire so I can show you exactly how much I want you."

He didn't wait on her response. Braden stepped out of the mess of comforter and tugged the blanket toward the fireplace. As he spread it out, he thought for sure he heard her shifting behind him. She wouldn't deny him or herself. That longing look in her eyes, the way she was speechless and flushed were all telling signs of what she was afraid to admit aloud.

He stilled when her hand settled on his shoulder blade. Slowly, as if to drive him completely out of his mind, she started trailing her fingers over his bare skin. She was tracing his ink, and he wasn't about to turn around and stop her no matter how much he wanted to see her, touch her. He meant it when he'd told her she was in control.

Even though he only wanted something physical from Zara, he still wasn't about to prove to her that he was like the other men she wasted time with. He would put her needs first, let her know she mattered here and what was about to happen didn't have to be ugly.

"Why did you get this?" she asked as she continued to trace the pattern. "I always wonder why people choose certain images to mark their skin for life."

On this he could at least tell her the truth. "It's a symbol that has deep meaning to my family. It dates back to the sixteenth century."

"It's beautiful," she whispered.

He couldn't wait another second. Braden turned, causing her hand to fall away, but the loss of her touch was made up for with the sight of her standing before him completely bare, completely giving and completely trusting.

"We need to set some rules," she told him.

Braden snaked an arm out around her waist and pulled her flush against his body. From chest to knee they touched, and there was no way in hell he was going to start in on some ridiculous conversation now.

"To hell with the rules."

He crushed her mouth beneath his. Zara stiffened for a second. Then, as if she couldn't deny herself anymore, she wrapped her arms around him and returned the kiss. Her passion came alive, bursting on to the scene in ways he hadn't experienced before.

She matched his desire, raising the bar to a level all her own, and Braden was the one who was nearly brought to his knees. He allowed his hands to roam over her, wanting to memorize the feel of her body, wanting her to get used to his touch because he planned on doing a whole lot more.

Braden eased back from the kiss, ignoring her protested groan which turned into a moan when his mouth traveled down the column of her throat and continued lower.

She gripped his hair as he palmed her breasts. Arching

her back, she silently offered herself up to him. Braden's lips covered her breast as he lowered her to the floor. He couldn't get enough of her, not her gasps, not her kisses, not her touch. He wanted it all, and willpower and trying to hold back were going to be a struggle.

"Do you have protection?" she asked.

Braden froze. Considering he'd only come here in his party attire, he hadn't planned on getting lucky that night. Damn it.

A smile spread across her face. "Go to my nightstand."

Thankful she was prepared, Braden made a mad dash to the drawer and found what he needed. Also thankfully, the cat stayed out of sight.

By the time he'd stepped back to the comforter, Zara was practically on display. Her arms on either side of her head, hair fanning out all around her. But it was those eyes that watched him so cautiously that made something twist in his gut. She may be trusting him with her body, but she was still not letting him in.

That fact should have given him a sense of relief, considering he was technically using her, but it didn't. He didn't want to just be some prick who proved to her that all guys were jerks.

But when she reached her arms out to him in a silent invitation to join her, there was no way in hell he could deny her or himself. Consequences be damned. Yes, this started with the scrolls, but the moment she'd walked into his office he'd wanted her, and he refused to feel guilty now. Allowing feelings to override what he was literally aching for would just leave a void that only Zara could fill.

Braden reached for her hand and settled down beside her, propping himself up on one elbow. While he wanted to devour her all at once, he also wanted to take his time, because this was a one-time thing and he wanted to savor every single second.

Trailing his hand up and down her abdomen, watch-

ing her muscles contract beneath his touch and hearing her
swift intake of breath, had him appreciating the fact he was
practicing that self-control now. He had a limited supply of
it and was using it all up on her, on this moment.

Braden watched her, studied her. He wanted to know
what she liked, what she responded to. The moment his
hand started trailing down her stomach, her lids fluttered
closed, her legs shifted in response and he was damn near
crawling out of his skin.

As his fingers found her most intimate spot, he captured
her lips, swallowing her moan. Zara's arms wrapped around
his neck, her hands sliding up into his hair, holding him
still…as if he would be anywhere else.

Braden eased back, enough to get protection in place,
before he settled between her legs.

"Don't look away," he commanded. "Your eyes are only
for me."

Why the hell did he want her to be so focused on him?
Why did he have that overwhelming primal feeling to keep
her all to himself?

Because he was selfish. Plain and simple and for right
now, Zara was his. He wanted to leave an imprint in her
mind of this moment and have her compare every single
man to him. He wanted to ruin her for others…and if he
thought too much about that, he would scare the hell out
of himself.

Braden pushed all other thoughts aside as he joined their
bodies. When her eyes closed, he shifted to his elbows,
using his hands to frame her face as his lips hovered over
hers.

"Only me, Zara."

When he started to move, she held on to his shoulders,
keeping her gaze on his. "Braden," she whispered.

Hearing his name on her lips as he filled her only exac-
erbated this unwanted emotional ache.

The second her body started pumping against his, her

face flushed, and Braden slid his mouth over hers, pushing her even further. Her fingertips dug into his shoulders as her body tensed. Braden lifted his head, wanting to watch her as she peaked. With Zara's head thrown back, a sheen of sweat covering her face and neck, Braden couldn't resist gliding his lips over her heated skin as she came undone around him. As he gripped her hips and tasted the saltiness of her skin, his own body started to rise.

Her trembling slowed, and Braden rested his forehead against hers. "Zara," he whispered, wanting her name to be the one he cried out, needing her to know he was fully aware of the woman he was with, that she mattered.

Before he could delve into that too much, his control broke. Braden covered her lips with his, wanting to join them in all possible ways. Her tongue met his as he shattered. Wave after wave washed over him, leaving only one thought, one thing that mattered at that moment…and it wasn't his family or the scrolls.

It was Zara.

Zara didn't do regrets, and there was no way she was going to start now. How could she when her body had lit up and was still tingling? Was tingle even the proper verb? She couldn't pinpoint what her body was doing, but the thrill that kept pulsing through her had everything to do with the man whose body still covered hers. Those long, lean legs rubbed against hers, the coarseness of his hair tickling her, sending new sensations throughout.

Part of her wanted to get out from under him, to get dressed and go on like nothing happened. He was her boss, for crying out loud, and she'd been so clichéd as to sleep with him.

But the other part, the part of her that was still lit up with passion, wanted to lie just like this wearing nothing but the weight of a powerful man.

"I can hear you thinking." Braden's warm breath tickled her ear. He eased up, propping himself on his elbows on either side of her face. "Maybe you need a replay so you can relax."

There was no way she could replay anything that just happened because then she'd want more. She'd want him. Sex was one thing, but wants were an entirely different matter she couldn't afford right now...and not with this man.

Zara pushed on his shoulders and slid out from under him. "No replays," she told him as she gathered her clothes. She tried like hell to not think about the fact she was walking around naked in front of her boss, but after what they'd just done...

"Already running, Zara?"

She risked a glance over and wished she hadn't. With a wrist dangling over one bent knee and his other hand holding is body upright, Braden's intense gaze pinned her in place. She clutched her sweats to her chest as if she could use them as some sort of defense against feelings. Damn emotional womanly feelings. Why did this have to be the man to stir something within her?

"I'm not running," she said. "I'm getting dressed and checking on the cat that's probably peed all over my floor."

"The cat is fine, and there's no rush to get dressed." He came to his feet and crossed the space between them. Just like he had before they'd gotten intimate. Only this time, Zara backed up.

"Braden." She held up a hand, thankful when he stopped. "I don't regret what just happened, it was amazing, but we can't do that again."

"If you're going to pull the whole boss/employer card, we're past that." His kissable mouth quirked.

"Yes, we are," she agreed. "But we're done. Nothing more can come of this."

There. She'd had a fling, she wasn't having regrets and now they could move on.

Crossing his arms over his broad chest as if he hadn't

a care in the world, Braden shrugged. "I'd had the same thought, but then I decided that wasn't right. Why should we deny ourselves what brings us pleasure?"

Zara listened to him, processed the justification, but in the end, she knew she'd get hurt because Braden was the type of man she could fall for…if she would ever let herself fall. One and done was the only way she could justify this encounter.

"It's best if we stop here and try to live with each other until you are able to leave."

The muscle ticked in his jaw, and Zara wanted to take back her words, ignore all the warning bells going off in her head and wrap her arms around him and have him give her that replay he'd suggested.

"I'll do what you want, Zara." He stepped closer, so close she could see the flecks of black in his deep brown eyes. "I'll honor your wishes, but that doesn't mean I'll stop trying to convince you that we were good together, and now that we know all about each other's bodies, we could be even better."

Those promising words delivered by a low, sexy tone did not help her cause. She clutched her clothes and watched as he wrapped up in that damn comforter again. He picked his cell up from the accent table and threw her a smile.

"I'm going to call the sheriff's department and see when travel is expected to resume."

And he walked out the door. Now the cat darted from beneath the bed and slid across the hardwood, bumping into her feet, but Zara remained frozen in place, still naked, still holding on to her clothes.

Still wanting him just as much, if not more than she had before they were intimate.

What had she gotten herself into? Because now she had a sense of what it meant to belong, just an inkling of how powerful a bond with someone else could be.

Ten

"You've got to be missing something," Mac stated.

Yeah, common sense.

"I've searched the hidden areas," Braden explained for the third time. But Mac was understandably frustrated, as was Braden.

He felt utterly foolish with this damn comforter as he stood at the base of the steps. He watched the landing for any sign of Zara, but she was most likely still up in her room replaying everything that had just happened between them.

"I'm telling you, if they're here, they're well hidden."

Mac's sigh carried through the phone. "Maybe her grandmother sold some things before she died. Hell, I don't know. Put more pressure on Zara. We need this, Braden."

Yeah, like he wasn't aware of that. "I'm doing what I can. Pressuring Zara will only make red flags go up."

"Is she suspicious of you?"

"No."

How could she be? He'd snooped either in plain sight of

her or when she'd been sleeping. And the fact that he still needed to do more searching and his time was running out only irritated him even more because, while he wanted to find the scrolls, he wanted to go back upstairs and talk Zara into spending the entire day in bed.

"Damn," Mac muttered. "Tell me you're not actually falling for this woman."

Braden gripped the wad of comforter and sank down on to the bottom step. "I'm not."

"You don't sound convincing."

Braden gritted his teeth. "I'm not trying to convince you, so drop it."

"Keep me posted when you can," Mac said. "I changed my flight to next week. Obviously with the weather I'm not getting back to Miami anytime soon. And Ryker is stuck in London. He had a slight run-in with the cops."

Braden rubbed his forehead and cracked his neck. "Define a slight run-in."

"No charges were filed and the art is now in our possession. The rest of the details can wait."

"There will be no backlash on us?"

"It's taken care of," Mac promised.

At least one thing was going their way for now, but Braden wasn't giving up on his hunt for the scrolls. And he wasn't giving up on this need that only Zara could fill. He'd thought for sure she would be out of his system, but she was in deeper than ever.

"I'll text you if I find out anything," he told Mac. "Hopefully I'll be home by tomorrow."

"Don't come back without the scrolls."

Braden disconnected the call just as he heard Zara behind him. Jerking to his feet, he replayed the conversation he'd just had with Mac and was positive he hadn't said anything to give himself away.

She descended the stairs and barely threw him a glance.

"I'm just grabbing a notebook from the office. Do you want me to take any food back up?"

She continued by him without even stopping. So she wanted to put this awkward wedge between them? He could work with that. He could handle anything she wanted to throw his way.

"I'm fine. I'm going to head up and check on my clothes."

He didn't wait for her to turn around or reply. Shuffling back upstairs, Braden was eager to get out of this makeshift skirt because he was going to have to revoke his man card if he didn't get back into pants soon.

Once he was dressed, they needed to talk. Zara was closing back in on herself, and there was no way he was going to let that happen. He may not be the man in her life, but he wasn't about to let her think that her feelings, her emotions meant nothing. Whatever pricks had taken her to bed in the past had let her think less of herself. Most likely they'd been selfish, too, and Braden refused to be lumped with those guys.

Regardless of what happened after he left this house, he wanted Zara to know her self-worth.

Braden placed the comforter back on the bed, smoothing out the edges, and pulled on his boxer briefs. They were damp but better than nothing. His pants were still wet, so he turned them and placed them even closer to the fire.

He'd called one of his contacts at the sheriff's department before calling his brother. Apparently the road crews were working around the clock, but with the layer of ice beneath the snow, there wasn't much chance of getting out within the next two days because the temperatures were still hovering below zero.

Perfect opportunity for him to keep up his search and prove to Zara that they were good together in bed. He wasn't asking for her hand in marriage; he just wanted to enjoy her company while he was here, and who knew, maybe after he left.

He chuckled at the fact he was strutting around her room in his underwear. She may not find the matter funny at all, but it was. Braden was snooping like Ryker and seducing like Mac…a position he never thought he'd find himself in as head of the family.

As he took a seat on the bed and sent off a quick text to Ryker, the cat rubbed against Braden's ankle. Reaching down, Braden lifted the fur ball on to the bed and started stroking his back.

The kitten let out a soft purr and flopped over on to his back. Braden continued to show affection, and his mind started drifting. He had no clue what he expected from Zara. Somewhere along the way he'd gone from wanting to use her, to wanting the hell out of her, to wondering more about her and wanting to uncover those complex layers she kept so guarded.

But he couldn't let himself get too involved. He wasn't ready to start looking for "the one." What he felt for Zara had nothing to do with forever and everything to do with right now. When she'd actually let go, let him close, he'd seen a woman with pent-up passion. All of that desire she kept locked away was a shame. She deserved to be…

What? Used? Because that's where he was right at this point. He was using her and justifying it by saying they had a physical connection. But damn it, he'd never denied himself anything before and he wasn't about to start now. He still wanted Zara, but she deserved more than a man who wanted her in bed and to technically steal from her.

The bedroom door swung open, and Zara came in juggling an oversize box. Braden leaped off the bed and crossed the room, taking the box from her hold.

"Let me have it," he said when she hesitated to let go. "You carried this up the steps when I could've done it." Once he set the box down at the end of the bed, he turned back to Zara. "You should've asked for help."

Her eyes took in his body, and he couldn't help the instant male reaction. "Zara—"

Those heavy-lidded eyes snapped up to his. "You have got to put clothes on."

"If I thought you really wanted me to, if you weren't just looking at me like you wanted me again, I would throw on those damp things and put you at ease."

She stared for a moment before a bubble of laughter escaped her. "At ease? That's the last thing you're trying to do here."

When she tried to step around him, Braden moved to block her. His hands gripped her shoulders, and he tipped his head down to look her in the eye.

"You're even more withdrawn than you were before we slept together. Care to tell me what's going through your mind?"

Those bright eyes darted to his, then to the bed where the kitten lay stretched out. "I'm just trying to keep this from getting too awkward. Okay? We need to go back to boss/employee."

Braden released her, took a step back and nodded. "That doesn't mean I wouldn't have helped you with the box."

For now he let the subject drop, but he wasn't leaving anytime soon, and no doubt they'd revisit their status again. Whether he had clothes on or not, she was strung so damn tight no matter how he looked. And now that he'd had her in every way, he wanted her again. So much for getting her out of his system.

"What's in the box? I thought you were going down for a notebook."

She maneuvered around him and pulled on the folded flaps until they sprang open with a puff of dust. Coughing and waving her hand in front of her face, Zara turned to face him. "I've been putting off going through some of my grandmother's things. They've been boxed up for a while. Long before her death, she wanted to downsize, so she started packing things away and putting them in a storage unit. I only had them brought back so I didn't have to keep paying the unit fee. This house is more than big enough to hold all her things. I have no clue what all she's put away and I've been too busy to look through them. I figure now would be a good time since I'm stuck here. Maybe after I go through her stuff, I will start unpacking my own."

Braden heard every word, but he focused on the fact her grandmother had boxes packed away, and now they were back in the house. These boxes wouldn't have been in here during the search Ryker did. Did he dare hope he could uncover the scrolls that were somewhere so simple as packed away in a box?

Braden leaned forward, glancing into the box. "I can get the other boxes and bring them up here for you."

Zara knelt down on her knees and started sorting through the newspaper-wrapped goods. "They're actually down in the basement. And let me just say, if you think the first floor is cold, that basement is frigid."

Braden laughed, more out of his own anxiety and nerves over the potential in the basement, but Zara relaxed at his actions. "Tell you what, I'll go down and bring up more. You start going through this box."

She crossed her arms and rubbed them, most likely trying to get rid of the chill from being downstairs. "I hate to have you do that. I can get them later."

No way in hell was he backing down on this, not when everything his family had wanted could be right within his reach. "Which boxes am I looking for? Are they all needing to come up?"

"Now who's stubborn?" she asked, lifting her brows and smiling. "Fine, you can get them. They're on the far wall. I believe there's about five more. All the others are mine, but they're under the steps."

Braden nodded and barely resisted the urge to rush out

the door. Then he remembered he was wearing only his underwear.

Zara glanced up at him; her gaze roaming over his body only heated him even more, making him want to put those boxes on hold and give into that look of desire staring back at him.

"You're going to freeze your important parts off if you don't put something on."

His inflated ego took control as Braden propped his hands on his hips and grinned down at her. "Worried about my parts?"

"You'll be needing them again."

He continued to stare until her face flushed.

"With someone else, I mean. Not with me," she quickly added. "I just meant… Wipe that smug look off your face and put your damn pants on."

Laughing, Braden went over to check, and sure enough his pants were nearly dry except for the damp waistband. He could handle that. After dressing, he glanced at the items she was pulling out of the current box. So far just a few old pieces of pottery. Not the scrolls.

Maybe they were hidden in the basement. Maybe they were in the boxes he was about to bring up…not before he searched through them, though.

And if that was the case, if he did indeed find the centuries old treasures, he could finally give back to his family what they'd been searching for.

He could also pursue Zara with his full concentration, because the way she'd been looking at him moments ago— yeah, she wasn't over whatever they'd started, and he'd barely scratched the surface of all he wanted to do with her.

As soon as Braden was out the door, Zara blew out a breath. Mercy, but that man strutting around in his black boxer briefs was a sight to behold. He could easily put models to shame with that broad chest, those lean hips and those muscles…she'd felt every single one of them, and if she were totally honest, she wanted to again.

No matter what she told herself, no matter the common sense that normally kept her grounded, all she could think of was how amazing Braden would be if they actually took advantage of this situation and stayed in bed exploring each other.

But what would happen once the roads cleared and Braden went home? She'd work his party in a few weeks, and they'd be professional…sure. How could she watch him from across the room, knowing full well what an attentive lover he was while she should be focusing on the hors d'oeuvres and making sure the Riesling fountain kept flowing?

Zara closed her eyes and willed herself to gain some sort of control over her emotions before he came back. She needed to concentrate on sorting through these boxes. Who knew, with all of the antiques and treasures her grandmother hung on to, maybe Braden would be interested in some pieces for the auction house.

There. When he came back, they would focus on work and not the fact they were going to spend another night together. Granted, it didn't matter whether it was night or not—they'd had sex in the middle of the day.

Day sex. That was new for Zara. Not that she had some big grand arsenal of partners and experiences, but she'd always been a night, dark room, vanilla type. Maybe that's why she wanted to explore more with Braden. He'd awakened something in her, and she wasn't sure she could ignore it now. What else could he show her? Braden O'Shea was a full-body experience, that was for sure.

Zara shook her head, hoping to clear some of these crazy thoughts. She reached into the box and pulled out another paper-covered object. As she unwrapped the oblong container, she wondered what could be in this tube she'd never seen before.

Zara set the paper to the side and concentrated on the silver caps on each end. She pulled on one, then the other. Either they didn't open or they were seriously stuck. Whatever was in there was extremely light. She shook the tube, but nothing rattled.

"I forgot a flash—"

Zara turned toward the door just as Braden's eyes zeroed in on the container she held.

"Don't touch that." One second he was by the door, the next he was kneeling at her side, taking the tube from her hands. "Did you look inside?"

Stunned at his reaction, Zara stared at him and shook her head. "The caps are stuck."

He ran his hands over the outer shell as if he was dealing with the most precious of gems. She'd never seen this side of him. She could sit here completely naked, and he'd not even notice she was in the room. For a man who was hell-bent on seduction and succeeding rather well at it, he was completely focused on this container.

Which made her wonder, what the hell was in that tube, and why was he so mesmerized with it?

Eleven

Braden had no idea if he was actually holding one of the coveted scrolls. All he knew was he wanted to get inside this tube now, but he didn't want to break anything or cause damage. This container was old, not as old as the scrolls themselves, but he had no idea what they would be stored in at this point. And with the way the caps were so secured, they'd obviously been in place a while. Which only added to that layer of hope.

Holding on to the tube, he glanced toward the box.

"Anymore like this in there?"

Zara reached in but only brought out a wrapped vase that was rather valuable with familiar etching. He'd worry about the other treasures later, because if he was truly holding a scroll that dated back to the time of Shakespeare, that meant the others could be in the boxes in the basement.

Braden lifted the tube and pulled gently on one of the caps again. It was sealed good and tight. While he was maneuvering as cautiously as he could, Zara got up and went out the door. He had no clue where she was going or what she was doing; all he knew was he needed to get in this compartment right now.

Both ends were good and stuck, and all he could think of was how fast he could search the other boxes for more tubes and how quick he could get Ryker to look into this. Something akin to elation flooded him as he gripped this container. Could he have found what his father hadn't been able to? Could he finally bring these back to the O'Shea family? As head of the family, he felt the pressure to do what his father hadn't been able to.

His family prided themselves on their business, yet they hadn't been able to relocate their own inheritance after decades of trying. All the frustration and anger and stomps on their pride may finally be coming to an end.

They'd hunted down so many false leads over the years, but now Braden wanted to focus on the last point of origin. This house held the answers; he just had to know where to look, and he may have struck gold.

Braden held on to the tube and stepped into the cool hallway. Where had she gone? He called her name, waiting to hear her reply. Silence greeted him, but then she appeared at the top of the stairs with the kitten beneath her arm. Even though the little guy nestled against her, Zara still didn't look comfortable with her new friend.

Maybe Laney shouldn't get this kitten, after all. Perhaps Zara needed this bonding experience to get her to open up, to not be afraid of any type of a relationship. Animals had that effect on people.

"What were you doing?" he asked.

"You left the door open, and he darted out." She stopped before him and held the cat out to his chest. "You were too preoccupied with whatever is in that cylinder and didn't see him run out the door."

Braden winced at the harshness of her tone and knew he needed to come up with a quick cover so she didn't get too suspicious. He'd never expected her to be around when he found something of interest, so holding back his emotions hadn't crossed his mind.

"Sorry. Occupational hazard. Old treasures get the best of me."

She quirked a brow as if she wanted to argue, but didn't say a word as she brushed by him and went into the bedroom. Braden followed, closing the door and placing the cat back down on the rug. He immediately went to the paper and packaging beside the box and started swatting and playing.

"Did you get that open?" she asked, pointing to the tube.

"No." He needed to be careful how he approached this. The last thing he needed was for Zara to distrust him. "I'd like to have Ryker look, if you don't mind."

She shifted slightly, and her brows drew in. "Ryker is a friend of yours?"

"He's more than a friend." How did he even explain Ryker? Ryker was more of an experience than a person. The man was a force to be reckoned with. He butted heads with Braden more often than not, but the man was loyal to a fault. "If anyone can get into this and not do any damage to the container, it would be him."

Zara stared at him before her eyes darted to the tube in his hand. "What do you think is in there that's so important? It felt empty to me."

A paper wouldn't weigh much, and if this was indeed one of his family's scrolls, Braden wanted it to be opened without Zara present. Waiting to get this to Ryker would be a true test of self-control, but Braden had come this far; he wasn't about to destroy the tube by breaking it to get in.

"Old documents could be hidden," he told her. "You never know what you can find stored away. We've uncovered some pretty important things from all over the world when people thought containers were empty."

"I don't care if you take it to look in, but you'll let me know what's inside, right?"

"Of course." He refused to feel guilty about lying to her face. If the scroll was indeed inside, it would be of no use to her.

Well, she could sell it for a ridiculous amount of money, but the worth to the O'Sheas was invaluable. Braden was so hyped up on adrenaline with the possibilities, he could hardly stand still. He needed to contact Mac.

Braden set the tube on the side table by the door and pulled his cell from his pocket. He quickly shot Mac a text that he'd found an old tube, but couldn't confirm the contents.

"I'm going to head back downstairs." Braden glanced around the room, searching for the flashlight. "I'll get those other boxes."

"I'd like to talk to you about selling some pieces." Zara had taken a seat back on the floor and was wrapping items back up and placing them in the box. "I'm not sure how that works or even if you'd be interested for the auction house, but…"

She was back to being nervous. And to be honest, he was a bit nervous, too, because he had no clue how to proceed from here. He'd never been in this position before. Sex with women was something he'd always enjoyed, yet he'd never gotten emotionally attached. Casual relationships worked fine, but in his line of work, getting too close to someone was difficult. One day he wanted a family, but he truly had to find the right woman who would fit into his life…first he had to steer the business into a bit more legit territory.

But he kept feeling this pull toward Zara, a pull he'd not experienced with any other woman.

So why Zara? Why now? Did it all stem from needing to gain trust? He'd never had to rely on someone like this before. He'd never placed himself at the mercy of needing anyone; he purposely didn't leave himself vulnerable.

"I can look through whatever you want," he replied. "If

we agree on certain items, you have a few options we can go over."

She nodded, and the tension in her shoulders seemed to lessen as her body relaxed. "Good. I hate getting rid of her things, but at the same time, I can't keep everything."

Braden knew that ache, that need to hang on to possessions of lost loved ones. He'd still not gone through his father's belongings and he wasn't sure when he'd be ready to face that daunting task. Mac and Laney weren't ready, either. Thankfully, they were all there for each other because family meant everything to the O'Sheas. They clung to each other in times of trial. Ryker may be a hard-ass, but the man was just as much family as any blood relative, and he'd grieved right along with the rest of them after Patrick's death.

"Let me get those boxes, and we can spend the day looking through them and deciding where to go from there." When she smiled up at him, Braden had to ignore that punch of lust to the gut. She was trusting him…and he was betraying her. "Be right back."

Before he could be swept under by those mesmerizing eyes, he snatched the flashlight off the bed and headed back to the basement. Right now he needed to focus on what they would uncover, on how this could possibly end his family's hunt for what was rightfully theirs. He couldn't think how Zara was slowly getting under his skin, how she was softening toward him and opening and driving him out of his ever-loving mind.

Because if he started letting Zara have control over his mind, she'd start silently taking control over other aspects of his life. And he couldn't afford to be sidetracked right now. Not when he was so close to getting everything he'd ever wanted.

Zara ran her fingers over the pewter picture frame. "I remember this picture sitting by her bed."

The black-and-white photo of a young, newly married couple stared back at her. Her grandparents on their wedding day, standing outside the courthouse because they hadn't wanted to wait for a big ceremony in a church. They'd fallen in love and hadn't wanted to spend another minute apart.

Tears pricked Zara's eyes. "Sorry," she said, smiling as she blinked back the moisture. "I get a little sentimental when it comes to my gram."

Sitting with his back against the headboard on the bed, Braden stretched his legs out as he stared down at her. Zara sat on the floor, legs crossed, looking through yet another box. Every now and then she'd pass a piece up to him to get his opinion on selling, but now she'd found a box of photos.

Braden extended his hand toward the picture, so Zara passed it over. "My grandfather was the love of her life. She never quite got over his death, even though she lived without him for nearly twenty years."

Braden studied the picture, then glanced back down to her. "And you still don't believe in true love?"

Zara rolled her eyes and swiped at the tear that escaped. "I believe my grandparents found it, but my parents sure as hell didn't. They were more concerned with making money and traveling than they were with love or family."

Propping the photo up on the nightstand, Braden adjusted it so it faced at just the right angle. "Love exists, Zara. If you want it, you just have to wait until it finds you."

Zara had always been sure that if she ever heard a man mention love, she'd run fast and far because he only wanted something from her.

This wasn't like any scenario she'd planned in her mind. For one thing, Braden wasn't professing his love by any means. Second, even if he was, he couldn't use her for anything. He was an O'Shea. One of the most powerful families in Boston and known around the world. There was nothing he could gain from getting involved with her.

"You're unlike any man I've ever met," she told him, trying not to think too hard about how amazing he looked taking up so much space in her bed. "I don't know many men who are so open at discussing love and relationships, let alone a man who claims he's wanting a wife and marriage."

"Family is everything to me. I want kids and a wife." He shrugged as if the explanation were so simple and not to be questioned. "When I find the woman for me, I'll do anything in my power to keep her safe and to make sure that she knows she's loved at all times. My woman will never question where I stand."

The more he spoke, the more stern he became. Zara knew without a doubt that he believed love existed, and she also believed there would be one woman who would come along, capture his attention and live happily ever after because she truly didn't think Braden failed at anything he set his mind to.

"Well, there is one lucky lady in your future."

Zara pushed off the floor and scooted the box to the wall. Turning, she scanned the other unopened boxes and finally decided on one that wasn't marked. Grabbing it, she took a seat at the foot of the bed on the opposite side. She faced Braden and pulled the lid off the box. Breath caught in her throat as she reached in and ran her hand over the silky yarn. Slowly, she pulled the crochet item from the box.

Zara smiled as she laid the bright red throw across her lap. "I remember when she made this," Zara murmured, running her fingers across the tight weave. "She'd asked me what color she should make, and I told her red. I remember thinking she was such a lively woman, brown or gray wouldn't do. When she was finished, she held it up and wrapped it around my shoulders. I was sitting on the couch doing homework."

Zara pulled the piece up to her face and inhaled. That familiar vanilla scent she associated with her grandmother hit her hard. A vice gripped her heart as she willed back the emotions. The bed dipped just slightly before a hand settled on her bent knee.

"It's hard losing someone you love, someone you've depended on."

His soft words washed over her, offering comfort when she really had no one else. How pathetic had her life become that she slept with her boss and had no close friends to turn to for support? Had she seriously alienated herself because she'd been so engrossed with work?

No, she could admit the truth to herself. Commitment terrified her. Being dependent on someone, knowing they could leave at any moment and take her heart with them had her refusing to allow herself to open up to anyone. She didn't care if she was lonely. She'd rather be alone than broken.

Dropping her hands back into her lap, Zara lifted her gaze to Braden. He'd been so passionate earlier, so attentive to her needs sexually. But now he looked at her with care and compassion, and she truly had no idea what to think of him or even how to act. He could make her want things… things she'd never wanted before.

"This is all so strange to me," she admitted. "Before I started working for you, I'd heard rumors of how badass you were. Then I saw it firsthand when you threw Shane out of the party. Then you take in a kitten, snuggle with it, for crying out loud, and you look as if you want to hug me, and not for anything sexually related. I'm not sure which Braden I'll see from moment to moment."

His eyes hardened, his jaw clenched, but he didn't remove his hand. "The badass Braden trumps the nice one. I'm not a nice guy, Zara. I'm selfish, and I take what I want when I want it."

Shivers raced through her. He'd taken exactly what he'd wanted where she was concerned…not that she was complaining.

Zara covered his hand. "You're a nice guy when it counts. You'll never convince me otherwise."

He looked as if he wanted to say more, but he eased back and slid off the other side of the bed. She watched as he surveyed the boxes littering her bedroom.

"So you only have one more to go through," he stated as he headed for the largest box he'd brought up from the basement. She knew he was changing the subject, which had been her tactic all along. "It was heavy, so you may want to come over here to look through it, or I can pull out items and bring them to you."

Zara swung her legs off the bed and headed toward the box. "Let's see what this one has, and then we can discuss what I'll be selling."

Because the tender moment that had just happened couldn't happen again—clearly it had left them both shaken. She needed to keep her wits about her and remember that she was still his employee, she was still needing this reputable job to keep her business going in the right direction, and she needed to forget how this man made her body tingle in ways she never knew possible…and how he was acting as if he truly cared.

Twelve

They'd had a gourmet dinner of crackers, lunch meat, cheese and some fruit. Zara had grabbed a bottle of wine from the cellar, and now she sat on the chaise, legs stretched before her, her back against the side arm as she twirled the stem of her wineglass.

The poor kitten was going stir-crazy, so Zara had taken him for a walk through the house. Braden was already seeing their bond form, but he wasn't about to call her on it. She'd realize soon enough.

As the kitten pounced on her shoe, Zara watched him. "Should we give him a name or something?"

"Does this mean you're keeping him?"

Zara threw Braden a look. "I didn't say that. I just feel like he should be called something other than *Cat*."

Braden laughed. "Admit it, you like him."

"I'll call him Jack while he's here," she decided.

"Jack?"

Zara nodded. "Jack Frost."

Braden smiled at the perfect name. "Jack it is."

Zara didn't want to make commitments, didn't want to have to worry about anyone else but herself, and Braden understood her reasons. But at some point she'd have to put herself out there, even if it was with a cat. She was going to be one lonely person if she kept herself so distanced. He wouldn't know what he'd do without his family.

"So, what's it like having siblings?" she asked, staring into her glass…her fourth glass if he was counting correctly. "Being an only child sucked sometimes."

Braden shifted his back against the side of the bed, brought his knee up and reached out to pet Jack as he came over and slid against Zara's leg. Braden had stopped at three glasses of wine. He was a big guy, so he wasn't feeling anything, and one of them had to keep their wits about them. Apparently that responsibility fell to him.

"We had our moments," he admitted. "Laney is the baby, and she gets a bit angry when Mac and I look out for her. She's determined, stubborn, always putting others first, even at the sacrifice of her own happiness." He narrowed his gaze, which he knew she could see since they had lit candles and she was only a few feet away, staring right at him. "Sounds like someone else I know."

Zara took a sip of wine. "I prefer career driven."

Braden laughed as went on. "Mac and I tend to get along now, but when we were younger we pretty much caused havoc in the house. Mom passed when I was ten, Mac was seven and Laney was only four. That was about the time Ryker started coming around, too."

Propping her elbow on the arm of the chaise, Zara rested her head in her hand and settled the base of the wineglass in front of her, still holding on to the rim with those delicate fingers. "You speak of him quite a bit. You all are really close. I can hear the affection in your tone when you talk of your family."

When she discussed her parents, all that had laced her

tone was disdain. The only love he heard from her was when she told stories of her grandmother.

"We've always been a close family. My parents were adamant about that. We may fight, yell, even throw a few punches, but when it comes down to it, I know my family always has my back, and they know I always have theirs."

Zara smiled. "Unconditional love." She drained the rest of her glass, then sat it on the small accent table on the other side of the arm. "I bet when you all were younger you had snowball fights in weather like this."

Braden nodded, his hand stilled on the kitten's back as he replayed one particular day. "My brother, Mac, has a scar running through his brow as a souvenir from one of our snowball fights."

Zara's eyes widened. "He got cut from snow?"

"He got cut because our sister threw a snowball that had a rock in it. She's a lot stronger than she looks, but she had no idea about the rock. Trust me, she felt awful, and Mac played on her guilt for years."

She made a soft noise of acknowledgment, nearly a tender tone that had him almost hating how he was reliving these memories when she didn't have too many happy ones. But she wanted to hear them, and he actually enjoyed sharing stories of his family…so long as people didn't start butting into the family business and asking unnecessary questions.

"I bet you all had a big Christmas tree, family vacations, huge birthday parties."

"Yes to all of that," he confirmed. "The downfall of the siblings, when you're a kid, no matter what you got for a present, you had to share. I never liked that rule. When something belongs to me, it's mine for good."

Zara's lids lowered a touch, from the alcohol or from the double meaning she'd taken from his words. Had he subconsciously said that just for her benefit? Maybe, maybe not, but he wasn't sorry now that the words were out.

"This morning, when we…you know…"

"Had sex," he finished when she trailed off. He had no clue where she was going with this, but he knew exactly what topic she was dancing around when she couldn't even say the words.

"Yes. I didn't handle that very well." Her fingertip toyed with the binding running along the outer cushion; her eyes remained fixed on his, though, which only made her sexier, to realize that she wasn't afraid to face this head-on.

"I don't know," he amended. "I think you handled the sex perfectly."

A flirty smile spread across her lips. "I meant afterward. I'm not used to such a giving lover. I didn't know how to react, and with you being my boss, I thought it was easiest to just ignore everything and try to pretend we were on the same level playing field as before we stripped out of our clothes."

Braden didn't say a word. The wine was apparently making her more chatty than usual, and now that she was discussing the proverbial elephant in the room, he wanted to know what she had to say.

"I guess I should've said thank you," she added quickly. "Circumstances have us here together, and you could've been selfish, you could've totally ignored me after, but you didn't. You were…"

"If you say nice I'm going to be angry."

"Sweet."

Braden groaned. "I would've rather been nice."

He eyed her for another minute, more than aware of the crackling tension that had just been amped up in the past two minutes.

"I'm trying to thank you," she went on, talking louder to drown out his mumble. "It's refreshing to know there are guys like you out there."

Guys like him? He wanted to laugh, he wanted to confess just how ruthless he truly was and he wanted her to never look for a man like him in the future. Yes, he'd been caring in bed; yes, he'd rescued a cat. Those were qualities any man should possess. Braden didn't go above and beyond. For one thing, her pleasure brought him pleasure. Call it primal, territorial, whatever. When Zara had been turned on, that made him all chest-bumping, ego-inflated happy because he'd caused her arousal, her excitement.

"Does that mean you're looking for a guy who will treat you right, and you're done with the asshats you've been dating?" he asked.

"Maybe it means I want you to show me again how a woman should be treated."

Braden froze. The bold statement slammed into him. Nothing much could catch him off guard, but this woman kept him on his toes.

"Your wine is talking," he stated, attempting to blow it off, give her an out in case she hadn't meant to say that aloud.

"Maybe so," she admitted. "Or I'm just saying what I've been thinking all day. Every time I'd look at you or accidentally touch you, I'd think back to how amazing this morning was. Even though a relationship would be a huge mistake, I'm finding it rather difficult to stay over here while you're in my bed."

Had the heat cranked up more in here? Braden was sweating after that speech she just delivered.

Zara stretched out even more on the chaise and rolled on to her back, staring up at the ceiling as she continued to talk. "Wanting you isn't new, though. You know what you look like. I'm sure women throw themselves at you all the time. I don't want to be that typical, predictable woman."

"Baby, you're anything but typical and predictable."

Her soft laugh wrapped him in warmth. "I'll take that as a compliment and I like when you call me baby. But I meant that I wanted you when I first saw you, but this job had to take precedence and I refused to be so trite as to hit on my boss."

Oh, he would've loved had she come into his office that first day and had her way with him. Before his fantasy carried him away too much, Braden concentrated on her as she continued.

"Then I was mortified you had to see that whole incident with Shane, but when you and I were dancing, I wasn't thinking about Shane. I was thinking how great you smelled, powerful and manly."

Braden smiled into the dim light. She would be so embarrassed tomorrow when she woke and realized all she'd verbally spewed out tonight. But there was no way in hell he was stopping her.

"Now that you're stuck here, all I can think about is how amazing this morning was and how I'm going to lie here tonight and replay it in my mind."

Braden came to his knees and slowly closed the space between them. He laid a hand across her abdomen, startling her as she jerked to stare him in the eyes. Their faces were inches apart, so close he could ease forward just a touch and have that mouth beneath his in seconds. From this closer vantage point, he could see the slight flush in her cheeks from the wine, the moist lips where she'd licked them from being nervous, the pulse point at the base of her neck.

"Who said you had to lie here and replay it?" he asked, easing his hand beneath her shirt. His palm flattened out on her stomach, and the quivering beneath his touch only added to his desire for her. "Maybe that bed was lonely last night. Maybe I got sick of rolling over and inhaling your jasmine scent. Maybe I was awake all night wondering when you'd come to your senses and join me."

Zara lifted her arms, her hands resting on either side of her face. The innocent move, or maybe not-so-innocent, arched her back and pressed her breasts up.

"I couldn't join you, Braden. I don't have a good track

record with men, not that I'm looking for one right now, and I couldn't risk my job no matter how much I wanted you. Besides, I would've died had you rejected me."

That right there was the crux of her issue. Rejection. She'd been rejected by so many people. Well, maybe not so many in quantity, but definitely all of the important people, save for her grandmother. She feared rejection, and here he was using her. Taking advantage of a vulnerable woman was a straight ticket to hell.

"I wouldn't have rejected you," he murmured. "I was battling myself back at my party because I just wanted to drag you into a room, a closet, anywhere that we could be alone, and I could show you how much I wanted you."

He trailed his fingertips over her heated skin, earning him a swift intake of breath as her eyes drifted closed. "That wouldn't have looked very good for my reputation," she muttered. "I'm a professional and I can't afford for people to think I slept with you to get the job."

"Nobody will think that," he assured her. He'd make damn sure she had more jobs lined up than she could handle. He'd make sure she could choose the ones she wanted and didn't have to worry about taking them all.

"Keep touching me, Braden." Her voice, a throaty whisper, washed over him. "Your touch feels so good."

She was killing him. Those soft moans, her body all laid out on display. He'd told her he wasn't a nice guy and he was primed and ready to snap and take what she was blatantly offering. But he wouldn't want anyone else treating Zara disrespectfully. She deserved better than a man who couldn't control his hormones and took advantage of the fact she loved wine and couldn't hold it like the rest of his Irish family.

"Zara." He stilled his hand to get her attention, to let her know he couldn't take her to bed. But her soft snore greeted him. Braden sat back on his heels, kept his hand on her stomach and simply stared.

When was the last time she'd fully let go and relaxed? Did she trust anyone in her life on a personal level, or were all of her acquaintances the closest things she had to family and friends? Dating men who were users, jerks and not looking for commitment was a surefire way to keep yourself closed off from the world. Zara was excelling at being a loner. The irony wasn't lost on him that she planned parties and lavish bashes for people to mingle, socialize and enjoy the company of others, yet she refused to put herself in a position to enjoy anyone.

From the investigating he'd done before hiring her officially, he'd learned she'd had a small apartment in Boston, mostly kept to herself and rarely dated. She threw herself into her work, and it showed, but wasn't there more to life?

Braden snorted. Yeah, there was, and he was going to find it as soon as his family business was a bit more secure in a new territory.

As he watched her sleep, something shifted inside him. He didn't want that damn shift. He didn't want to care so much about Zara, about her loveless childhood and how it molded her into the fierce woman she was today.

All Braden wanted to do was wake her up, take her to bed and make love to her all night. Then he wanted to get home tomorrow and show Mac that tube so they could figure out how the hell to proceed from here.

Yet none of that was going to happen, so here he sat staring at the most complex, beautiful woman he'd ever known. Parts of her reminded Braden of his sister. He hadn't been feeding Zara a line of bull earlier when he'd said that, either. But Laney had something Zara didn't, and that was the strength and backing of a family.

It bothered him more than it should that Zara had nobody. He'd been fully aware of her living situation and family life before he'd hired her. He'd made a point to know exactly who Zara Perkins was so he could come at her the right way, the way that would ensure she trust him, work for him and allow him access into her home.

Granted, he hadn't planned on a snowstorm, but he wasn't looking a gift horse, or Mother Nature, in the mouth.

Braden sighed and raked a hand through his hair. He should rest, he should get back up and start searching. But he didn't want to do any of that. Not when Zara's body felt so warm beneath his palm, not when she was sleeping so peacefully and beautifully.

For once, he wasn't thinking work or how to get those coveted scrolls. No, for once Braden O'Shea was soaking in all of the goodness from another, hoping it would somehow rub off on him and make him not so much of a bastard. Because if Zara ever found out what he'd done, she'd hate him forever.

And that chilling thought scared the hell out of him.

Thirteen

Zara rolled over onto her side, coming to rest against a warm leg just as her arm crossed over a taut chest. She stilled, blinking into the darkness. No candles were burning, but the soft glow from the logs helped her get her bearings. She wasn't on the chaise where she'd been drinking her wine.

Wine. Zara froze. She'd gotten pretty chatty if she recalled correctly, but thankfully she was still dressed. So nothing had happened between Braden and her, but she was lying in bed beside him. Had he put her here?

Zara slowly started easing back to her side instead of crawling all over her temporary roommate.

"And here I thought you wanted to touch me."

Braden's thick tone filled the room.

"I didn't mean to… I had no idea we were…that you were…"

Lightning fast, Braden grabbed her arm and held her still. "Don't move. I put you here because I want you here."

Zara had to admit being in her own bed with her feather-down duvet was like heaven. Okay, fine, she loved being next to this man, knowing that he carried her and put her in bed, then climbed in beside her. What woman wouldn't get all giddy over that fact?

"Did I ask you to have sex with me again?" Mercy, the fact she had to even ask that question was even more embarrassing than the actual question.

"You implied you were willing."

Pathetic, party of one?

"Which just proves my theory that you're a nice guy."

In an instant, Braden had her on her back, her hands above her head, the entire length of his body on hers. "Do you feel light-headed at all? Headache? Dizziness?"

Breathless from their current state, Zara shook her head. "Why?"

"Because I'm about to strip you and take you up on that offer now. I want you to be fully aware of what I'm doing to you."

His lips captured hers before she could even comprehend what he was saying, but words were moot at this point. The fierce kiss, the tilt of his hips against hers and the way he gripped her wrists above her head were all very telling signs as to what he wanted. Added to that, her body had lit up from within, and she wanted everything he was willing to give her. She wasn't denying herself, not now, not with Braden.

He was right. She dated jerks. She did so to keep a distance and not form any relationship. So why shouldn't she sleep with a man who was considerate, obviously wanted her and wasn't asking for any type of commitment?

Oh, right. He was her boss. Well, at the moment, her boss was removing her pants and panties right along with them. Even as Zara's mind told her to put a stop to this, her body shifted so he could continue ridding her of the unwanted clothes.

She kicked the pants off her ankles and groaned when

Braden placed open-mouth kisses on her stomach. She threaded her hands through his hair. She'd already slept with him once; stopping now wouldn't change what had already happened. And Braden's promise of stripping her down was already proving to be amazing because he currently had his teeth on the hem of her shirt, sliding it up her torso.

When the material bunched at her breasts, she tried to pull her hands free to help.

"I've got this," he whispered. "Your only job is to relax and let me work."

Who was she to argue? He was her boss, after all.

He eased back enough to jerk the shirt over her head and toss it to the floor.

"If that cat pees on my—"

Braden's tongue trailed down her throat and into the valley of her breasts, cutting off any thought she'd had. Zara's back arched—she couldn't move much with his weight on her, but she wiggled beneath him enough to let him know he was absolutely driving her mad with this slow pace he'd set.

"Braden," she whispered. "Please."

"Anything."

He cupped one breast, stroking her skin with his thumb, his other hand trailing down her side and settling on her hip. His mouth, his hands—he seemed to be touching her all over at once. Zara's legs shifted anxiously, waiting for his next move. How could he be so thorough when she just wanted him to touch her where she ached the most?

Finally he slid his fingertips over her thighs, inching higher. Zara tilted her hips, near ready to beg him for more when he finally covered her with his hand. She eased her legs wider, giving him the access he needed.

While his fingers stroked her, he moved his other hand to lace their fingers together over her chest. His lips slid over her abdomen, and Zara thought she was going to shoot up off this bed if he didn't finish her soon.

"You're squirming," he murmured against her stomach. "You're going too slow."

His soft laughter filled the room. "I'm hanging on by a thread trying to give you pleasure, and you're complaining."

Zara pulled her hand from his and framed his face, forcing him to look up at her. "Put us both out of our misery. I want you. Now."

Braden crawled up her body, leaned over to the nightstand and pulled out a condom, quickly sheathing himself. When he rested his hands on either side of her head and hovered right above her, Zara's gaze locked on to his. Something flickered in his eyes, something she'd never seen from him before…or any other man for that matter. Before she could read too much into it, he plunged into her, making her cry out.

Gone was the slow, patient Braden. This Braden had snapped, was staking his claim and pulling her into his web of passion and desire.

His lips trailed over her shoulder, her neck, up her jawline as he continued to pump his hips. Zara could only grip his biceps and arch into him because he was in total control and doing everything absolutely perfectly.

Perfect. That was the one word that kept coming to mind every time she thought of Braden and how they were together.

When he kissed her, roughly, passionately, all thoughts evaporated. Her entire body heated, rising higher and higher as he increased the pace.

"Braden," she panted against his mouth. "Braden… I…"

He kissed his way to her ear and whispered, "Zara."

Her name softly on his lips when his body was so hard, so intensely moving against hers was enough to set her over the edge. She couldn't control the tremors racking her body; she couldn't control the way she screamed his name, clawed his shoulders.

Braden's entire body tensed as he arched back. Clenching his jaw, he stared down at her as he climaxed. The intensity of his stare stirred something so deep within her, so deep she was positive nobody had ever even uncovered that area before.

But Braden had. He'd uncovered so much about her, even more than she knew about herself.

When Braden eased on to his back, pulling her to sprawl on top of him, Zara could no longer deny the fact she was falling for her boss. And she could say that with certainty because he was the only man to ever care, to ever put her first, to ever pull feelings from her she hadn't even known she'd possessed.

The best part was that he did every bit of that without even trying. He just…was. He was everything she hadn't known she was looking for, and here he was, holding her so tightly after he'd made love to her in her own bed. His heart beat against her chest, and Zara had never been more aware of another the way she was with Braden.

The question now was what did she do about these feelings she never wanted? They were too strong to ignore, they were too scary to act on, but she'd never backed down from fear before.

Now she just had to figure out how to be strong, keep her business with the O'Sheas and keep Braden in her personal life for good.

Braden woke to a sleeping Zara on his chest, her hair spread all around him. Something had happened in the middle of the night…something that had nothing to do with the sex. There had been a new level introduced. How the hell had that happened? He'd seen something in Zara's eyes and he knew full well it was more than desire, more than lust.

But what scared him most was what she may have seen in his own eyes. He knew what he'd been feeling when they'd been together. Even if he was only admitting it to himself, he was feeling more for Zara than just physical attraction.

Raking a hand over his face, he reached to the bedside table for his phone and turned it on. The battery was starting to get low, but as soon as the phone powered on, his texts lit up. Apparently the road level was downgraded, and he could get out now. Did he tell Zara, or did he continue to stay here and search her house? He'd found the one tube that could be holding a scroll and he desperately wanted to get it into Mac's hands.

The electricity was still out, but maybe the electric company would be coming through soon, since there were no driving restrictions now.

His entire home had a backup generator. Possibilities swirled around in his mind. Zara nestled closer to his side, a soft sigh escaping her lips. When her warm breath fanned across his bare chest, he knew right then that he would be going home today…and she'd be coming with him.

That primal, territorial need he had for her had intensified. The ache to see her in his home, in his bed was nearly all-consuming.

Braden shot off a quick text to Mac that he would be home later with Zara and the container. Yes, it was presumptuous to assume she'd be coming with him, but he wouldn't take no for an answer. He saw exactly how much he affected her, he felt it, and after last night, she may wake up more confused than ever; but until Braden knew what the hell was going on between them, he wasn't about to leave her alone to start thinking of all the reasons they wouldn't work.

Not to mention he didn't want her out of his sight until he learned what was in this tube, because if it did indeed hold one of the scrolls, he would have to search this house again.

Braden set his phone back on the nightstand and turned toward Zara, wrapping both arms around her. As he pulled her body flush against his, he couldn't help but wonder how he'd gotten so far into her world. He'd started with wanting to gain enough trust to get into her home, and while she'd interested him from the start, he'd be lying if he said he hadn't wanted to sleep with her; but no way in hell had he planned on getting emotionally involved.

Damn it. This complicated things.

"I'm getting spoiled," she mumbled against his chest. "Waking to a warm, naked man who's holding me. Not being able to work, eating junk all the time."

Braden raked his hands up her back, loving the feel of all that smooth, silky skin beneath his palms. "Get dressed. The roads are better so we're heading to my house."

Zara jerked back. "Your house? Are you going to ask or just demand? I'm fine right here, you know."

"My house has a backup generator, so we'll have full amenities." He kissed her temple, hoping to soften her even more. "You're more than welcome to stay here, but why don't you come with me until your house is up and running?"

She tensed beneath him, and he wasn't about to give her the chance to back out. Softly he covered her lips with his. "I want you in my bed, Zara," he murmured against her. "I need you there."

Knowing he was fighting dirty, he allowed his fingertips to trail back down. Cupping her bottom, he pulled her against his hips. "But if you don't want to join me, just say so."

Zara groaned. "You're not playing fair."

"I'm not playing at all." He nipped at her lips. "I have some work to do, but I promise we'll pick up right here later."

Her brows drew in slightly. "I don't know, Braden."

"I do." He rested his forehead against hers, knowing she needed tenderness. "If we didn't work together in anyway, would you come to my house?"

She hesitated.

"I'm not asking for anything more," he added. "I'm just not ready to let you go."

"You make it impossible to say no."

Braden laughed, kissed her softly and tipped her face up. "That's my plan. Now let's get dressed and get out of here."

As he rolled over and came to sit on the edge of the bed, the cat darted out and rubbed against Braden's ankles. His sister would definitely take this little guy in if Zara didn't. That girl took in so many stray animals, she needed to live out in the country where she had land for such things. Having a home in the middle of Boston wasn't ideal for a make-shift animal shelter.

Braden rubbed the cat's back before coming to his feet. He'd pulled on his boxers and pants when he realized Zara was still in bed, the sheet pulled up beneath her arms, covering all the delicious spots.

"What's wrong?"

She toyed with the edge of the pillowcase. "What will your family say about me coming home with you? I mean, they know me as the events coordinator. Are they going to think I'm... I don't know."

He wanted to put her uncomfortable state to rest and move on. "Just say it. What are you afraid they're going to think?"

Her eyes met his. "That I'm using you for this position."

Guilt weighed heavy on him, but he brushed aside the unwanted emotion and crossed back to the bed, taking a seat on the edge and reaching out for her hand.

"First of all, you were hired long before we slept together. Second, it's nobody's business what we're doing. And lastly, they would never think that."

Zara's eyes searched him as if she were trying to tell if he was lying or hiding something. He couldn't very well tell her his family would never think she was using him because he'd been the one to use her in the first place. She could never know the real reason he'd hired her new company. No way in hell would he want her hurt in such a manner.

Because even if the scrolls were discovered in this house, Braden wasn't so sure he wanted to give up seeing Zara.

Suddenly the quest for his family's heirlooms and the need to be with this woman were totally separate issues, both important and both he refused to back down from.

Fourteen

Zara walked through the hallway of the O'Sheas' home. Unlike the other night when she was working and in the ball-room, now she was on the second floor, following Braden to her room…which she had no doubt would actually be his room.

In one hand he pulled her suitcase, in the other he held the kitten. Everything about this seemed a bit domestic, a bit too personal. Yes, sex was personal, too, but what they'd shared last night had gone so far beyond sex, but she had no clue about the territory she'd entered and she couldn't spend too much time thinking on it or she may run screaming.

And had Braden asked her to come to his home when he'd been dressed and not rubbing all over her body, she could've used some common sense and told him this wasn't the smartest of ideas. She was safe staying in her house with the gas heater. She'd eaten just fine, thanks to the stash of Pop-Tarts, and she'd been warm. What more did she need?

Zara adjusted her laptop bag on her shoulder. Braden

had stepped into the house and promptly handed the mystery tube to Mac. They'd exchanged a look, and Zara knew they'd just had some silent conversation that only worked when such a deep bond was formed. She had no idea what was so important about this find, but whatever it was, she trusted him to clue her in since the item was from her grandmother's house.

"You can work in here." Braden stepped aside, gesturing for her to enter the room first. "There's a desk in the corner by the double doors. I need to speak with Mac, and I could be a while."

He pulled her suitcase over to the closet and turned to face her. "Will you be all right?"

Zara glanced around the spacious bedroom. The king-size bed sat on a platform on the far wall. The dark, rich four posters were masculine, matching the deep blue bedding. Of course a man like Braden would have his bed be the dominant feature in his master suite. The sitting area with leather club chairs and a mahogany coffee table only added to the overall masculine theme of the room.

"This is your bedroom." She didn't ask as her eyes met his.

Still holding the kitten in one arm, he crossed to her. Each step he took seemed to be in tune with her heartbeat.

"I told you this is where I wanted you. Nobody will bother you in here. The staff knows to stay away from my quarters, and Mac keeps a guest room on the other side of the house. We have total privacy here."

Zara shivered at the veiled promise, but at the same time, the prospect of being totally alone with him, on his turf where she may be able to learn even more about him, held so much appeal.

"Go on," she told him with a smile. "I'll be fine. I actually have several things to work on, and now that I don't have to worry about my battery, I can focus for several hours. Do you need to leave the kitten with me?"

Braden shook his head. "Nah. He likes me. Not as much as he likes you, but I'll let him run around for a bit." Stopping at the doorway, Braden turned, offering her a lopsided grin. "I'll have dinner brought up later. I plan on spending the entire evening with you and no interruptions, so make sure you get that work done because you're mine."

That man did have a way with delivering promises. The impact he could make on her body without even touching her was astounding. But she couldn't stand in the doorway all day and daydream about how sexy and amazing Braden was.

For one thing, she wasn't moving in. She was here temporarily, and she needed to remember that. For another, she was behind on work. She had to get her spreadsheets updated for the upcoming events, Braden's included. In the next two months, she had seven events planned, some big, some small, but Zara prided herself on treating each event as if it was the only one she worked on. She wanted her clients to feel special, to feel as if she cared only for them and no one else.

Zara headed to the antique desk in the corner near the doors that led out on to a balcony. The thick snow blanketed the open space, but Zara's imagination worked just fine. What she wouldn't give to work on a terrace during the warmer months. How inspiring and refreshing to be outside on the days she worked from home.

Once she booted up her computer, she tried not to focus on the giant bed directly across from her line of sight. If she stared too long, she'd start fantasizing even more about what would take place there later, and since she already knew how talented the man was in bed, her fantasy just sprang into mind without her even trying.

Zara closed her eyes and sighed. She seriously had to get a grip on this situation and her feelings. Right now he was downstairs working with his brother, and Zara needed to remember she had a job to do, as well. The weekend was over. Even though the snow still covered a good portion of the area in Boston and the surrounding towns, Zara still had to think ahead. When these upcoming events rolled around, the snow would most likely be gone, and her clients were expecting a spectacular party.

Zara pulled up her schedule and made mental notes as well as jotting down some handwritten ones. She did nearly everything online, but still reverted back to pen and paper at times. She might do some things old-school, but that was okay. She attributed those skills to her grandmother.

And thinking of her grandmother brought her mind back around to Braden and what he'd found, if anything, inside that tube.

"Damn it." Braden slammed his fist on the desktop. "Where the hell did it disappear to?"

"You don't even know one of the scrolls is what was in here." Mac carefully put the cap back on. "There were no other tubes?"

Braden rested his palms on his desk and shook his head. "Nothing. There were still some boxes, though. Zara hadn't even unpacked her own things, yet. Between all of that and her grandmother's things, I could've spent days searching that house."

Standing on the other side of the desk, Mac laid the tube down and crossed his arms. "You were there for two days, and from what I can tell you managed one empty tube and sleeping with the woman you're using. You're in quite a mess, brother. We'll get the scrolls eventually, no need to seduce your way to them."

Fury bubbled within Braden. He leaned forward, holding Mac's gaze. "Don't be an ass. What Zara and I do is none of your concern, and I'm more than capable of searching. I know my position here."

Mac smiled, completely uncaring as to Braden's building anger. "Sounds like your lady's gotten to you. Why don't you just tell her what you want? At this point she trusts you. You guys played house for two days, you brought back a damn cat and now she's up in your room. If you tell her you need to search her house, I doubt she'd turn you away."

Braden pushed off the desk. He couldn't tell her. Not now. It was because she trusted him that he couldn't come clean with what he needed. Once she discovered he'd lied from the beginning and only initially hired her so he could get close, she'd start to question everything between them, and he couldn't have that.

"I'll find another way," Braden assured Mac. "When will Ryker be back?"

"He made it back to the States, but the airport is closed. He flew into Provincetown and rented a car. He should be here this afternoon."

Turning to face the floor-to-ceiling window facing the snow-covered property, Braden racked his brain on a solution. He'd been so damn sure there was a scroll inside that tube. He had to focus, keep his head on straight or he'd find himself in an even bigger mess. He was the O'Shea in charge now, and he needed to damn well act like it.

"Ryker needs to get into Zara's house while she's here," Mac stated simply.

"No." Braden shook his head, tossing his brother a glance over his shoulder. "I won't do that."

Damn it. What had happened to him? Three days ago Braden would've jumped at the chance to have Zara here preoccupied in his bed while Ryker went through her house. But now...well, now he couldn't go through with it.

"You're falling for her."

Braden jerked around. "I am not."

"I can't blame you," Mac went on as if Braden's denial meant nothing. "She's beautiful, sexy, a businesswoman. Clearly everything you'd ever want in a woman."

Yeah, she was. That was part of the problem, because he couldn't take things to the next level with her. For one thing, he'd only just gotten to know her, and when he said he wanted a wife and a family, he meant it. He didn't just want a woman to keep his bed warm. Braden wanted that bond his parents had. But the obvious reason Zara couldn't be that woman was because he'd lied to her from the get-go. Braden wanted a wife, a family, yes. But he wanted it to be the real deal, and there was no way he could start a relationship with someone he'd lied to, was continuing to lie to.

And how the hell had his mind gone into wife mode when he thought of Zara? That was ridiculous. She didn't do relationships, and he was using her. Definitely no happily-ever-after for them.

"Don't get carried away." Braden rounded the desk, pulling his phone from his pocket to check his messages. "Have you heard from Laney?"

"Yesterday I did. I guess Carter is staying with her during the storm."

Braden grunted as he scrolled through his email. "I need to take a shower and change from these clothes. Once Ryker gets here we all need to have a meeting."

Mac nodded. "And what about your houseguest?"

Braden gripped his phone and eyed his brother. "She's not your concern."

"You know she's going to find out what's going on. You've brought her here, she's going to hear talk or get suspicious as to why you want back in her house."

Gritting his teeth, Braden was well aware of all the concerns in having Zara here, but he wasn't ready to let her go.

"You let me worry about Zara," Braden warned. "Once Ryker gets here, we'll work on a plan. I'd be more comfortable if Laney was here, too, but she's stubborn."

"Carter wouldn't let her come."

Braden laughed. "The day that schmuck keeps my sister away from me is the day he disappears from her life for good."

Mac nodded in agreement. "I'll text her and tell her I'm

having Ryker pick her up on his way here. She needs to be in on this meeting anyway."

"Give me fifteen minutes. We'll just meet in here. I'll have the cook prepare a late lunch for us."

Braden headed toward the doorway, then stopped and glanced over his shoulder. "Don't argue if Laney acts like it's a problem to come. Ryker will take care of any issues. Just text him."

Mac laughed. "You know Laney and Ryker are like oil and water, right? Are you wanting a fight? It's best if I try to run interference before he gets there."

Braden shrugged. "I trust Ryker to take care of it, and Laney will know why we need her here. It's none of Carter's business, and I don't give a damn if Ryker offends him."

"Our little sister is going to arrive, and I'm pointing her in your direction when she unleashes her anger."

Braden thought of the woman currently upstairs in his bedroom. "I can handle an emotional woman." He hoped.

Fifteen

"I didn't need to be manhandled by the family bouncer."

Braden sat behind his father's old desk, now his, and looked across to his sister who refused to take a seat. With her arms folded, she shot death glares between Braden, Mac and Ryker. She may not be happy, but she was here.

"If you'd just said we needed to have a family meeting, I would've had Carter bring me," she continued, zeroing in on Braden. "I don't appreciate being told I was coming and my ride would be Ryker."

The man in question leaned against the wall by the door. His thick arms crossed, he'd yet to take his coat off, and he'd not said a word. Braden knew the man was processing everything, but he also didn't have a care in the world...least of all an angry Laney.

"Carter isn't invited to my house." Braden eased back in his chair and met his sister's fiery gaze. "I know you like him, but I don't, and you're well aware of my feelings on that matter. Ryker was coming in from the airport, and it was easier for him to get you. Now, are you going to have a seat or stand there and pout because you don't like your mode of transportation?"

Laney narrowed her eyes. "It's the lack of respect I'm pissed about."

"I respect you, Laney." He smiled when she finally took a seat next to Mac on the leather sofa. "If I didn't, you wouldn't have been called to this meeting."

Braden glanced up to Ryker. "Close that door."

Once the door was closed, Ryker moved on into the room, sinking into the oversize leather chair next to the sofa. Braden eased forward, resting his forearms on the desk.

"We'll discuss what happened with you in London later," Braden promised, nodding to Ryker. "First, we need to discuss the scrolls. I've spent the last two days in Zara Perkins's home, and so far all I've found is an empty tube that may or may not have held one or all of the scrolls. I'm sure they're stored separately, because together they could be ruined."

Laney shifted, leaning onto the arm of the sofa. "Did she know you were looking?"

"No. We were going through some of her grandmother's boxed-up things, and that's when I found this tube."

He pulled the container from below his desk and sat it up for them to see. "I was unable to get it open, but when I brought it back, Mac managed to get into it. There was a miniscule section that looked as if it had been broken before, so he pried that part open."

Ryker was first to reach for the tube. He examined it thoroughly before resting it on his leg. "Tell me where you looked in her house, and I'll start my search in other areas."

Because Ryker assumed he'd be the next plan of action. He never questioned his duties, his position. He'd been the muscles, the enforcer, the behind-the-scenes man for the O'Sheas for years. Braden knew Ryker felt an intense sense of loyalty because he'd been taken in when his home life was extremely lacking.

"I don't want you going in again," Braden countered, earning him raised brows from Ryker. "Zara trusts me, and I don't want you going into her house while she's here."

"You've got to be kidding me," Laney stated, eyes wide. "We need to find these and get them back where they belong. Either tell her what's going on or let Ryker look. And what the hell is she doing here?"

Braden ignored Mac's smirk. "She's staying here until her power comes back on, and that's all you need to know."

"So you're sleeping with her, and you've earned her trust, you say, yet you can't ask her to have a look around?"

That pretty much summed up his predicament, but he wasn't going to get into this with his baby sister. Whatever was going on with Zara was private.

Besides, the guilt that slid through him was getting quite uncomfortable. He was using Zara, no way to sugarcoat that. If any man treated Laney like this, Braden would destroy him.

"She doesn't have to know," Ryker chimed in. "I'm quick and thorough."

Mac eased forward to face Ryker. "Braden has suddenly developed a conscience where his woman is concerned."

Angry that his credibility was coming into question, Braden fired back at his younger brother. "Would you betray Jenna?"

Mac's eyes narrowed. "Jenna is my best friend, nothing more. I've known her for years. And, no, I'd never betray her for any reason."

"Then shut the hell up, and let me handle this."

Raking a hand over his face, Braden truly had no idea how to deal with the situation. "The scrolls may not even be in the house at this point. They could've been moved or accidentally tossed out. But, I have to believe had they been sold, we would've heard about it. Documents with Shakespeare's earliest works would've hit the media worldwide. Even if sold on the black market, we would've heard whispers. Our reach is far enough in the underground world."

"So how are you going to search the house?" Ryker asked.

"When I take Zara back home, I'm going to find a reason to stay." That wouldn't be too hard, considering their current state. "I'll search where I haven't. I won't leave anything untouched. I don't want to lie to her any more than necessary, so we're not breaking in."

"And what are you going to do if Zara finds out you've lied to her?" Mac asked.

"She won't find out," Braden assured him. She couldn't find out, because if she did, all this work would be for nothing. Not only would she permanently block him from searching, she'd never trust again. He'd made so much progress in only two days, he refused to believe anything bad would happen. And it was a risk he was willing to take to get all he wanted.

Zara had become too important too fast. He wasn't ready to sever their personal tie. Scrolls aside, he wanted her. And, if he told her even a portion of the truth, she was so distrusting that he wasn't sure she wouldn't cut him out of her life. She had every right.

"The cook has prepared a late lunch," Braden stated, coming to his feet. "I need to speak with Ryker privately."

Mac and Ryker stood, but Laney remained seated, stubborn as ever. "And when can I go home?" she asked.

"Whenever Ryker wants to take you."

Ryker glanced to Laney. "Might be a while. I still need to eat and crash. I had a bit of a run-in with the London police, and I'm jet-lagged."

"I'll call a cab," she said through gritted teeth.

"No, you won't," Ryker commanded.

Braden bit the inside of his cheek to keep from smiling. Mac turned his head to hide his smile, as well. Ryker could go without sleep for days. He was a force to be reckoned with, and if he wanted to do something, he'd do it. Apparently he didn't want Laney to leave yet, which was fine with Braden. The more she was away from Carter, the better.

Before Laney could protest, because she no doubt would, her cell rang. Pulling her phone from the pocket of her jeans, she glanced at the screen, then up to Braden. Without a word, she came to her feet and moved to the opposite side of the room where she answered with her back to them.

"You know he's calling to check up on her," Mac whispered.

Braden nodded in agreement. "I don't see what the hell she puts up with him for."

"She's defiant." Ryker's eyes remained on Laney. "She may see something in him, but she's staying with him out of spite because you two make a big deal about it."

Braden eased a hip on his desk and crossed his arms. "And you don't? I'm sure you didn't get out of her house without a verbal sparring match with Carter."

Ryker sneered. "I can handle that prick."

"I don't know when I'll be home." Laney's slightly raised voice carried across the room. "Of course I'm at my brother's house. Where else would I be?"

Braden's blood boiled, and a little of what Ryker said started to ring true. Maybe in Mac and Braden's attempt to protect her, they'd driven her deeper into the arms of a controlling asshole. Damn it. He needed to talk to her one-on-one.

Mac headed for the door. "I'm getting something to eat. I'll be around if you need me."

Braden pulled his gaze from his sister and stepped closer to Ryker. "Do I need to know anything about London?"

Ryker's dark eyes met his. "I handled it."

"With no trace back to us?"

Nodding, Ryker's jaw clenched. "I even managed to gain

the trust and cooperation of two of the boys in blue. Next time I go back, we'll have no worries."

Relief slid through Braden. He knew whatever Ryker had done, he'd done his job well. "And the item is secured?"

"It's in the Paris office, ready to go back to its rightful owner."

Braden slapped Ryker on the back. "Go eat. I'll clean things up with Laney and take her back home."

Ryker's brows lifted. "You're taking her back willingly?"

"She makes her own decisions. I'm just hoping she sees Carter for who he is before it's too late, because if he crosses the line more than he has, he'll have bigger problems on his hands than just checking up on her."

Ryker's thin lips pulled into an eerie grin. "I'll take her back after I eat. I'd like to have a talk with him."

Braden shook his head. "I'll take care of it. You go relax."

Ryker looked as if he wanted to argue, but finally he nodded. After throwing Laney one more glance, he left the room.

While waiting for her to finish her call, Braden put the tube in the lock cabinet by the door. He didn't want that container going anywhere for now.

Finally Laney turned, slid the phone in her pocket and started toward the door. Braden stepped in her path and hated that look of sadness that stared back at him. While he wanted to unleash his anger and tell her to drop that jerk, he knew she wouldn't listen to words.

In a move that surprised both of them, Braden glided his arms around her shoulders and pulled her against him. He kissed her on the head and whispered, "I'm sorry I was a jerk to you."

Laney squeezed him back, resting her head on his shoulder. "You're always a jerk, but you never apologize."

Laughing, Braden eased back and smoothed her dark hair away from her face. "I just want you happy and to be with someone who deserves you. I just don't like how Carter treats you."

"He treats me great when we're together," she said with a slight smile. "His ex cheated on him, and he's leery. I can't blame him after hearing the stories."

Braden would save his opinion on that topic. From the rumors he'd heard, it wasn't Carter's ex doing the cheating at all. But Braden still had a tail on Carter, so time would tell.

"You can stay and eat, or I'll take you home. Whatever you want."

Laney tipped her head and narrowed one eye at him. "Who are you and what have you done with my big brother?"

He shrugged. "I told you, I just want you happy."

Her features softened as she ran a finger between his brows. "Your worry lines aren't as prominent as they normally are. If I had to guess, I'd say Zara is to thank for the new Braden."

"Zara is…" Hell, he didn't even know what to say.

Laney patted his cheek. "It's okay. I can tell your feelings for her are strong, and I won't say a word. Just promise me you won't hurt her. I don't know her personally, but if you're having these emotions, then I'd say she is, too. Be careful where your hearts are concerned."

Braden swallowed and feared that when all was said and done, someone's heart would be hurt.

Ignoring that lump in his throat, he looped his arm through Laney's. "Why don't you stay and eat? Then I'll take you back."

Laney looked up at him with bright eyes. "I love you, Braden. Dad would be proud of you."

Another point that worried him. He hoped like hell he did the O'Shea name proud, because his father, grandfather and great-grandfather had done an impeccable job of building up a reputation. Some may be skeptical, but the name was respected and sometimes feared. No one messed with the O'Sheas. And once Braden guided the family into an even more reputable area, he could hold his head high, knowing he'd done the right thing.

Braden led Laney toward the kitchen. Once he got her back home, he could focus on Zara. Their time alone couldn't come soon enough.

Sixteen

Braden was surprised when he stepped into the master suite and Zara was nowhere in sight. A hint of her signature jasmine perfume lingered in the room.

He turned toward the attached bath and smiled. Looked as if she was a step ahead of him. He undressed as he moved toward the wide doorway. His shirt fell off his shoulders to the floor, he stepped out of his shoes, hopped out of his socks and shed his pants and boxers. By the time he stepped into the bathroom, he was more than ready to join Zara.

But he stopped as soon as his feet hit the tile. There in the sunken garden tub was Zara. She'd apparently packed bubbles because she was neck deep into them, her head tipped back, hair piled on her head and eyes closed. Was she sleeping? She wasn't moving.

Braden took a few moments to take in the sight of Zara relaxing in his tub. He'd never used it, never had a need. He grabbed a shower and that was it. This sunken bubble bath never looked so good.

Damp tendrils clung to the side of her neck, her pink lips parted on a soft sigh. Braden could barely restrain himself. He'd never wanted a woman with such a fierce ache before, and the knot in his gut told him this need wasn't only physical anymore. If everything between them were merely physical, Braden would've let Ryker go into her place and look around. But he couldn't do it.

Zara shifted, her eyes opened, instantly locking on him. A slow, seductive smile spread across her face.

"I meant to be done by the time you came up. But this is too relaxing." She lifted one bubble-covered arm, reaching out to him. "Join me?"

Braden wasn't about to turn down an invitation like that, even if he'd smell like flowers when he got out. Being with Zara, no matter the circumstances, was totally worth it.

Zara scooted forward, giving him room to step in behind her. When his legs stretched out on either side of her, Braden pulled her back against his chest. She rested her head on his shoulder and peered up at him.

"Did you get your meeting taken care of?"

He scooped up bubbles and swiped them over her bent knees. "I did and now I'm all yours. Did you manage to work?"

"I added another event," she stated, her voice lifting with excitement. "Parker Abrams was at your party the other night. His assistant sent me an email about working on his corporate event he hosts once a year for his employees. Apparently their last coordinator was caught making out with Parker's intoxicated son. Great news headline, bad for business. But how am I any different? I'm sleeping with my boss."

Braden smiled. "That's great news for you. I promise to keep our fling a secret."

Her lids closed, and Braden wanted to take back the words. This was starting to feel like more than a fling. He knew it, even if he didn't admit it out loud. There was something deeper than intimacy going on here. Short-term was the only way he'd worked before, but now…he didn't necessarily want to keep Zara a secret. She deserved more… they deserved more.

Zara rubbed her hand along the arm he had wrapped around her stomach. "I feel weird discussing business with you when we're naked. It's wrong…isn't it?"

Nothing about this moment was wrong. Nothing about having Zara smiling, happy and naked was wrong.

Braden nuzzled against her neck. "Then maybe we shouldn't talk."

Zara's slight groan had him reaching up to cup the side of her face, turning her so he could capture her lips. But the woman in his arms went a step further and turned until she faced him. Braden straightened his legs when she straddled his lap.

"I was lying here dreaming of you," she told him as she poised herself above him. "I have no idea how we got to this point, but I don't want to be anywhere else."

Encircling her waist with his hands, Braden stroked her damp skin with his thumbs. "I don't want anything between us, Zara."

"I've always used protection, and I'm on birth control." She tipped her hips, enough to nearly have his eyes roll back in his head. "What about you?"

"I'm clean and I've never been without a condom."

She quirked a brow in silent question. Braden eased up enough to claim her mouth at the same time he thrust into her. That instant friction, skin to skin, no barriers, was so new, so all-consuming, he wanted to take a moment and just…feel.

But Zara started moving, starting those pants as she tore her mouth away and gripped his shoulders. When she tipped her head back and bit her lip, Braden was absolutely mesmerized by the woman who'd managed to have complete and total control over him. So much so he was letting her into his private life, into his home. He'd never brought a woman into his bed.

Zara was different. He'd known it from the moment she'd stepped into his office. And now she was his. Would he ever let her go?

The thought of losing her chilled him, but he refused to think on that now.

Braden slid his hands up her soapy sides and cupped her breasts. Sliding his thumbs back and forth earned him another groan as she arched her back.

"Look at me," he demanded. He needed her to see him, to see them. Every primal part of him suddenly took over. "You're mine."

Those wide eyes locked on to his, and her mouth opened in a silent cry as he quickened the pace.

"Say it." Braden went back to gripping her waist, holding her still so he could gain back control. "Say you're mine, Zara."

"Yes," she cried. "Only yours."

When his hand dipped in the water and touched her intimately, she shattered all around him. Braden would never tire of seeing her come undone, of knowing he caused her pleasure. This was his, she was his. No other man would experience Zara so long as Braden was around, because he wasn't kidding and he hadn't been swept into the heat of the moment when he'd demanded she say she belonged to him.

Just as her trembling stopped, Braden squeezed her waist and let himself go. Zara leaned down, whispering something into his ear. He didn't grasp what she was saying; it didn't matter. This woman in his arms was all he needed for tonight, for tomorrow.

And now Braden was starting to wonder if she was the woman he needed forever. If she was, how the hell would he ever be able to build on anything when their initial meeting was all based on a lie? On him using her?

As Zara lay spent against him, Braden knew one thing

for certain. He either needed to let her go once he searched her home, or he needed to come clean with how they'd met in the first place.

Either way was a risk. Would she understand? Would she see that he'd had no choice in the matter, but once he'd gotten to know her all bets were off?

She had to understand, because Braden refused to lose her. Having her walk away wasn't an option.

Someone smacked her bare backside.

Zara jumped, twisting in the silky sheets and thick duvet. Sweeping the hair out of her eyes, she glared up to see Braden staring down at her, a wicked grin on his face and a twinkle in his eye.

But he was holding a cup of coffee. "That better be for me," she grumbled, reaching for the mug. Jack clawed at the side of the bed until Braden lifted him up.

"Of course. I also managed breakfast."

He reached to the nightstand and presented her with a plate. Zara eyed it before pulling the napkin from the top. A laugh escaped her.

"I know full well you do not stock s'mores Pop-Tarts in your house, considering you hadn't had them before I introduced you to them." She plucked one off the plate as she took a sip of the steaming hot coffee, black, just the way she liked it. "So how did you manage this?"

He cocked his head and raised his brows as if her question was absurd. Of course he had someone go out in this ridiculous weather just to get her a box of Pop-Tarts. The idea warmed her more than it should. It was a box of processed junk that cost a couple bucks, but he'd done so out of…what? Love? No, he didn't love her, but he obviously cared for her.

"Hurry up and eat," he told her. "I have another surprise for you."

With the Pop-Tart between her teeth, she narrowed her

eyes and bit off a hunk. Jack stretched out on Braden's pillow next to Zara. "What?"

He stepped back from the bed, and she took in the sight of him wearing—a ski suit?

"I hope you brought warm clothes. If not, I'll find something for you. Laney most likely has some clothes in her old room."

"Where are we going?" she asked, a bit nervous at how energetic he was this morning. Apparently the two times he'd woken her in the middle of the night hadn't worn him out.

"Just eat, put on warm clothes and I'll go see what else I can find." He leaned down, kissed her on the forehead and eased back just enough to look her in the eyes. "Trust me?"

Zara swallowed, nodded. "I wouldn't be here if I didn't."

Something flashed through his eyes, but just as quick as it appeared, the image was gone. Braden nodded down to her plate. "Eat up. You're going to need your energy."

"After last night, I'm exhausted."

His mouth quirked up in a grin. "Compliments will get you everything."

Zara rolled her eyes. "Easy there, tiger. Your ego is showing."

"My ego is never hidden," he countered as he walked to the door. "I'll have a heavier coat and thick gloves for you downstairs. Meet me by the front door in twenty minutes."

Zara gave him a mock salute, which earned her a chuckle as he walked out and closed the bedroom door behind him. She had no clue what he had planned, but obviously something outside. Was Braden an outdoorsy type? What did she truly know about the man she was falling for?

She broke off another piece of her pastry and smiled. She actually knew quite a bit. He was loyal and he was caring, though he'd never admit it. Family meant everything to him, and he wanted his own one day. He may have a reputation as a hard-ass, a man to be feared in the business world, but the Braden O'Shea she saw was loving.

Zara finished her breakfast and coffee, then set her dishes on the bedside table. She unplugged her phone from the charger and checked messages. Then she wished she hadn't. Three texts from Shane asking if she was all right. The first one was a simple question, the second was more demanding and the third was flat-out demanding. Arrogant jerk. Without replying, she laid her phone back down and started getting ready for...whatever it was she was doing this morning. She had emails to get to, but for now she wanted to be with Braden because he'd gone to the trouble of surprising her, and he seemed excited. Zara didn't know if she should be scared or worried.

The sooner she got dressed, the sooner she'd find out what Mr. O'Shea had planned.

Seventeen

"You're kidding."

Bundled up like an abominable snowman with layers upon mismatched layers, a bright yellow cap on her head and red snow boots, Zara stared at Braden as he knelt down in the knee-high snow and started forming a ball. The man may be a ruthless businessman, but this playful side was just as sexy and appealing.

"Do I look like I'm kidding?" he shot back over his shoulder. "We're building a snowman. Get down here and make balls."

Zara snorted. "You're going to freeze yours off," she muttered.

"Cute. Now help me."

Surveying the pristine blanket of snow, Zara squinted her eyes at the glare from the sun's reflection. She shoved her gloved hands into the pockets of Laney's old ski coat. Apparently she'd had some old things in her closet, and Braden claimed his sister wouldn't care.

Zara wasn't sure what had her more scared, the fact that she was getting in deeper with this family or that Braden was showing her his playful side.

It was the snowman. Something so simple, so traditional hit her right in the gut.

Braden glanced back over his shoulder, then pushed to his feet. "You're frowning."

"You probably did this all the time growing up," she stated, looking at the mound he'd started. "It's ridiculous how something like this freaks me out."

Braden stepped closer, peered down at her until she met his gaze. "You're supposed to be having fun. I want you to experience all the simple things, and I want to be the one to experience them with you. For now, we're starting with a snowman. Maybe later we can make snow cream or have hot chocolate with little marshmallows."

What did he mean he wanted to be the one to experience things with her? Was he thinking long-term? Was he saying he wanted something permanent?

"Where are we going with this?" she asked.

Braden braced his hands on her shoulders. "Wherever we want." He nipped at her lips. "But right now, we're making a snowman, and we're going to have fun. Then I'm going to kick your butt at a snowball fight."

Zara laughed. "You can try, but don't take inexperience for weakness."

"Is that a challenge?" he asked.

"Consider yourself warned." Zara took in a deep, cool breath and sighed. "Now, let's get to making some big balls."

Laughing, Braden smacked another cold kiss on her lips. Together they worked rolling one giant ball. Zara had no idea building a snowman was so much work. Despite the twenty degree temps, she was actually starting to work up a sweat. By the time they got the third ball rolled and on top of the middle one, Zara was nearly winded. Her muscles were hurting, and for mercy's sake she was clearly out of shape. Apparently eating junk and planning parties didn't help build up the endurance.

And here she thought her running regimen kept her endurance up. Apparently, she needed to change her workouts to walking in deep snow and using her core to keep her balanced.

"I'm going to need to soak in that tub again," she told him as they stood back to admire their work. "My muscles are crying."

The wicked grin he shot her sent shivers of arousal coursing through her. "I could be persuaded to give you a massage."

"During the bath?"

"I'd say we both deserve to soak our tired muscles."

Zara glanced back to the snowman. "This thing doesn't look finished. Should we have a carrot or something?"

Braden laughed. "I brought out a bag of various things. It's on the porch."

As he maneuvered through the snow to the porch, Zara got the most wonderful idea. Before he could turn back to see her, she quickly made two snowballs. Compact in each of her palms, she held them until just the right time.

The moment he turned around with the bag in his hand and stepped off the porch, Zara pelted him right in the face. She couldn't even fully enjoy his look of shock because she was doubled over with laughter and trying to gather more ammunition.

Before she could straighten, a wet, cold blob smacked her on the side of her head, barely missing her exposed cheek.

Zara tried to get to the snowman to use as a shield, but she ended up slipping in the snow and falling headfirst into the snowman, sending it toppling.

"No," she screamed as her body landed on the head.

Braden tackled her from behind. "That's what you get for fighting dirty."

He rolled her in the snow and pinned her down. She couldn't catch her breath for laughing. Braden straddled her as he trapped her hands beside her head.

"Still laughing?" he asked. "You may have got the jump on me, but who's in charge now?"

"It was worth it." Zara attempted to control herself, but his face was wet from the snowballs that had assaulted him. "I'm sorry I killed our snowman, though."

"You don't look sorry. You look smug."

"And you look cold," she countered. "I guess I kicked your butt at the snowball fight since you only got my hat."

Braden leaned down, his lips hovering just over hers. "You know what they say about paybacks," he muttered before he kissed her thoroughly, passionately…promisingly.

She hadn't even noticed he released her hands until icy cold snow was shoved into the top of her coat.

"Braden," she yelled as he jumped off her. "You put snow down my top."

She hopped up, dancing around, trying to get the blistering snow off her bare skin. "That's not playing fair."

"I gave you a warning about paybacks," he called as he scooped up another snowball.

Zara ducked as the ball flew over her head. "Oh, buddy. It's on."

Soaking in the garden tub had definitely done wonders for the sore muscles. Not to mention the fact Braden took full advantage of massaging every inch of Zara before he made love to her.

After their epic snowball fight, which they finally declared a tie, they came back in, and thanks to the chef, who was now going to get a raise, Braden and Zara had steaming cups of hot chocolate with marshmallows. Braden hadn't even had to request the treat.

Now they were spent in every way as they lounged beneath the covers in his massive bed.

"You're going to make it hard for me to go home," she muttered, snuggling deeper against his side. "Besides the hot sex, I've been undressed so much here, I may never want to wear pants again."

Braden's hand slid over her bare backside. He wasn't ready for her to leave. "Fine by me. Keeping you in my bed won't be a hardship."

Zara trailed her fingertips over his taut abdomen. "It's going to be a bit unprofessional of me to host parties while naked in your bed."

"You'll definitely be remembered."

These past few days had been more than he'd ever thought possible. Zara had embedded herself so deep into his life, he needed to come clean because he wanted to build something stronger, something permanent with her.

Once he explained why he'd needed to get into her house, she'd understand. They'd forged a bond so intimate and so fierce, he knew she would understand. Her grandmother had meant the world to her, so that family loyalty she would be able to relate to. Even though her parents hadn't been the most stellar of people in her life, Zara would see where he was coming from.

Then they could discuss the future. He just wished like hell his hand hadn't been forced, because he didn't want to tell her he'd lied to her. Right now she looked at him as if he were everything she'd been searching for but afraid to hope for. He didn't want to be the one to disappoint, to crush her and make her untrusting again.

"I need to tell you something." The words were out before he could fully gear himself up for this talk. "I'm not sure where to start."

Zara stilled against his side. Damn it, he hadn't meant to start out like this, instantly putting her on the defensive.

"You've asked before where this is going." Braden shifted to his side so he could face her. Lying in bed wasn't the ideal place to start this, but she was naked so she wouldn't run out angry. "I don't want you just in my bed, Zara. I want more."

Her eyes widened, either in panic or in shock he wasn't sure.

Reaching for her hand, he brought it to his chest and held her palm flat over his heart. "I know this has been fast, but the attraction was there the moment you came into my office. Seeing you at the party the other night only intensified things. But spending so much time with you over the past few days, I've realized that I care for you more than any woman I've had in my life other than my sister and my mother."

"Braden." Zara closed her eyes. "I want this, so much. But everything about long-term scares me. I mean, I can't even unpack all of my clothes at my new house. I want things, I want stability and a foundation. I've just never had that in my life, and… I'm scared."

Her words came out on a whisper, her breath tickling his bare chest, her declaration slicing him in two.

"I know you are, and that's why I want to be completely honest with you." Damn it, was that him trembling? "You're the woman I want in my life because you make me want to be honest, you make me want to be that guy you trust and think is such a good person."

Zara slid her hand from beneath his and eased back. "What do you mean be honest?"

"There's so much you need to know, and I have no idea where to start."

Braden sat up, rubbing his hands over his face. He was either the stupidest man alive or he was brilliant for coming clean like this and risking her trust. Surely once she learned the truth, the truth that came straight from him, she'd understand. Finding out any other way would make him look like a jerk, and understandably she'd be pissed. But by confessing his sins straight to her, Braden was confident she'd forgive him and they could move forward.

Could things be that easy?

Her hand rested on his shoulder blade. "Braden. You're scaring me."

Yeah, he was scaring himself, too. But this was worth it; *she* was worth it.

"My family has had some priceless heirlooms missing for decades." He opted to start all the way back at the beginning as opposed at the end when he'd started using her. "We had an ancestor who was an Irish monk during the sixteenth century."

"I have no idea how this affects us," she stated, coming to sit up beside him.

"Just listen."

Braden turned, facing her because he'd never backed down from what he wanted, and he was facing Zara head-on because he'd never wanted anything more.

"My ancestor transcribed nine of Shakespeare's works and they were written on scrolls. They were passed down from generation to generation, but during the Great Depression they were in a house that belonged to my family. They lost everything and were forced out before they could get the scrolls."

Braden searched her eyes as he grabbed her hand. "Those scrolls were left in the house, and we've been searching for them since."

"I still don't get any of this," she told him, shaking her head. "What do these scrolls have to do with us?"

"The house that belonged to my family until the Depression is yours, Zara."

"What?" she gasped. "Wait a minute, you think I have some documents that supposedly have works by Shakespeare hidden in my home?"

He watched as she processed all the words, then her shock morphed into hurt right before his eyes. Before she even spoke, his heart clenched in pain for her. He never knew he could physically hurt simply because someone he cared for was in pain.

"Did you search my house?" she asked, agony lacing her voice as she scooted back from him and clutched the sheet up around her neck as if she needed a shield of protection.

Braden swallowed the lie that could easily slip out. He wasn't that guy, not with her. Not anymore. "Yes."

Her lips clamped together as moisture gathered in her eyes. "And helping me go through my grandmother's things. That was another way for you to search?"

He nodded as lead settled in his gut.

"That was why you flipped out when you saw me holding that tube." Her eyes darted away as she spoke, as if she were playing the day back through her mind and realizing what he'd done. "You were in such a hurry to get back here, you wanted that opened so you could see inside it."

"There was nothing in it."

Tear-filled eyes swung back to him. "So now what? You need to do another search? Why didn't you just ask me in the beginning?"

Another gasp escaped her seconds before a tear slid down her cheek. She didn't bother to swipe it away, and that wet track mocked him. He'd done this to her. He'd hurt her, on purpose, but he'd had no other way initially. Not only that, he'd justified his actions.

"You hiring me wasn't because of my abilities at all," she whispered, scooting back. "You were using me from the start."

Before he could defend himself—and what could he say that wouldn't sound terrible—Zara sprang from the bed and started pulling clothes from her suitcase.

"I've been such a fool," she declared as she pulled on a pair of panties. "You've been playing me for months. I refused to believe the rumors about your business, about how ruthless and conniving the O'Sheas are. Now I know the truth. I won't let you use me again."

Eighteen

Zara's hands shook—from anger, from hurt, from the urgency to get the hell out of here. She couldn't get dressed quick enough.

"You're not leaving."

Zara yanked a sweatshirt over her head. "If I have to walk home, I'm not staying with you another second. I refuse to be with a liar and a manipulator, with a man who claims to care for me, yet you lie about everything."

Braden stood, grabbed a pair of boxer briefs and jerked them on before coming around the side of the bed. "There's so much about my business I can't share with you, Zara. We do what we have to do, and, yes, we use people, we've lied, we've cheated. But everything you and I have shared was genuine and real."

"Real?" she cried as she turned to him, her hands propped on her hips. "How can anything be real when the trust was clearly one-sided? Do you know how hard I fought what was happening between us? I kept telling myself that we couldn't get involved, that anything I felt for you was all superficial. Your power, your charm, everything about you drew me in, and then you went and showed me that sweet, caring side that had my guard coming down."

Zara refused to give into the sting of tears. She blinked them away before continuing, because if he wanted honesty, he was about to get it.

"I believed everything you said to me," she went on, her tone softening because the fight was going out of her. "I believed every touch, every promise. The fact that you sought me out to purposely use me cuts me like nobody else's actions or words ever has. How did you plan on getting into my house once you hired me? Seduction? You succeeded. I guess this storm really played well into your hands."

Another thought gripped her. "Shane warned me your family were liars and manipulators. I ignored him because I thought he was jealous. Looks like he might have had my best interest at heart after all."

"Zara."

He started to reach for her, but she stepped back, bumping into the small table her suitcase laid on. She skirted around it, never taking her eyes off him.

"Do you think I'm going to let you touch me? You did this. You destroyed something I was starting to hope for, something I'd already settled into. Damn it, Braden, I was falling for you, and you betrayed everything good that I had in my life. My self-confidence, my business, us."

She let out a lifeless laugh at his pained expression. "There never was an *us*, though. There was you sneaking behind my back, using me, and then there was me being naive and hopeful."

"Would you listen to me?"

Braden took a step forward and came within inches of her. Zara refused to back up, back down. She would put up a strong front before him if it killed her. She could collapse later in the privacy of her empty home.

"The deceit started when I hired you for who you were. I can't deny that. And, yes, I wanted to find a way into your house by gaining your trust. But the moment I got into your house, the second I touched you intimately, something changed for me. I still wanted to find what I came for, but I also wanted you and not just in bed. You did something to me, Zara. I can't let you go."

He seemed so heartfelt, so genuine, yet none of that mattered because it all came down to the fact he'd lied and betrayed her.

"You have no choice," she retorted, crossing her arms over her chest to keep more hurt from seeping into her heart. "You should've come clean before you took me to bed, because now all I think is you slept with me to gain my trust. You manipulated me, used my feelings."

Zara glanced around the room and let out a sigh. Ignoring Braden, she pushed past him to gather her things from the bathroom. Her eyes darted to the garden tub where memories had been made. Never again would she be a fool over a man. She should've listened to her heart in the first place.

Grabbing her lotion, toothbrush, bubble bath and razor, Zara came back out and dumped it all into her suitcase. She didn't care if anything leaked over her clothes; she had bigger issues at the moment.

With a swift jerk, she zipped up her luggage and turned back to Braden, who still hadn't moved. "I want someone to take me home. Not you."

The muscle in Braden's jaw ticked as he nodded. "Ryker is still here. I'll have him take you."

Zara extended the handle on her suitcase and started for the door. When Braden reached for it, she shot him a look. "Don't touch it. From here on out, I need nothing from you."

Before she could open the door, Braden slapped his hand on it, caging her between the wood and his hard body. "I'm letting you walk away because you need to think about this, about us. But I'm not giving up on you, Zara. You know in your heart everything between us was real. You felt it in my touch. That's something even I can't lie about."

Zara closed her eyes, wishing she could stop his words from penetrating so deeply into her heart. He'd already taken up too much space there. Surrounded by his heat, his masculine scent, Zara needed to get out of here where she could be alone and think without being influenced by this sexy man…a man she'd thought had a heart of gold. He only proved those men didn't exist.

"Let me go," she whispered. "I can't be here. I can't do this. Romance isn't real after all, is it?"

When his hand settled on her shoulder, she nearly lost it. Because no matter what he'd done to her, she couldn't just turn off her feelings.

"Don't shut me out," he whispered against her ear.

Steeling herself against his charms, his control over her, she shifted so his hand fell away. "You shut yourself out."

"Let me get dressed and I'll find Ryker for you."

Zara threw him a look over her shoulder. "I'll find him. I've already told you from here on out, you're not needed."

Pushing away, she opened the door and headed out into the hall. She'd never met this Ryker Braden had talked about, but surely she could find him and get the hell out of here.

She'd wait outside in the freezing cold if she had to. It couldn't be any colder than the bedroom they'd shared.

Awkward was such a mild word for this car ride back to her house. And because the roads were still covered, the trip took twice as long.

Zara didn't dare glance over to her driver. The man was built like a brick wall with coal-black hair and dark eyes. She could easily see why he was the O'Sheas' go-to guy. He had that menacing, brooding look down perfectly. Fitting for being the right-hand man for a lying, cheating family.

And the scar running along his neck? The man had barely

said a word to her other than "hi" and "the truck is over here," but he had badass written all over him.

"I've never pried into Braden's personal life."

Zara jerked in her seat at the deep tone and the fact he was actually going to bring up the proverbial elephant parked in the truck with them. "Then don't start now," she countered.

"I owe him," Ryker said simply before continuing. "He's never brought a woman back to the house, so whatever is going on between the two of you, it's serious. The O'Sheas are a private family. Other than the parties in the ballroom, no outsiders come into their home."

And that told her more than she needed to know. They were all hiding something.

Zara stared out the window. "You may owe him loyalty, but I owe him nothing. He's a liar."

Silence enveloped them once more. Zara folded her arms, pulling her coat tighter around her. She couldn't get warm, and it had nothing to do with winter hanging on for dear life.

"What did he tell you?" Ryker finally asked. The cautious way he phrased the question put Zara on alert.

She turned in her seat to face him, no longer caring how menacing this man was. "I assume you know full well why he wanted in my house, since you're like a brother to him."

Ryker's silence told her everything she needed to know. She refused to discuss this further with a stranger—not only a stranger, but one who was devoted to Braden.

As they neared her house, Zara's anger bubbled and intensified. Not only had Braden lied to her, he'd had a whole damn team of people in his corner. She hadn't thought of this sooner, but no doubt his brother and sister knew, too. She'd been made a fool by the entire family.

Ryker pulled on to her street, rounded the truck into her drive and put the vehicle in Park. Just as she reached for the handle, he spoke up once again.

"I offered to break into your house while you were staying with Braden." Ryker's dark eyes met hers, holding her in place. "He refused because he didn't want to betray you anymore."

A lump formed in her throat. "I'm glad he feels guilty."

"That wasn't just guilt. You know exactly what he feels for you."

Zara didn't want to think about what Braden's true feelings for her were because he had a warped way of showing them. Added to that, was she seriously sitting here having a heart-to-heart chat with a man who looked like an extra from a mafia movie?

Jerking on the handle, Zara stopped. She wanted to keep the upper hand, she wanted Braden to know she was in control of her life. What better way than to call him on his betrayal?

Zara glanced back to Ryker. The man's intense gaze still locked on her.

"Come on in," she invited. "You want to know if those coveted scrolls are here. I have no idea, but if they are, they're technically mine since I own the house. But you're more than welcome to come and look."

"And if I find them?"

Zara shrugged. "Then it sounds like Braden and I will have some business to discuss."

Ryker eyed her another minute, and she didn't know if she was more afraid if he came inside or if he didn't.

Nineteen

"The hell you say?"

There was no way Braden heard right.

"She invited me inside to look around," Ryker repeated.

Braden sank down into his leather office chair and processed Zara's shocking actions. Ryker remained standing on the other side of the desk, the man never ready to fully relax.

"I didn't go," Ryker added. "Whatever is going on between the two of you is something I want no part of, and it's so much more than the scrolls at this point."

Braden didn't want to be part of this mess, either, but unfortunately he'd brought it all on himself and he was screwed.

"I'll take care of this," Braden promised. "You have more work to do. We have a piece in Versailles that needs to be acquired before the May auction, too. I have the specs here."

Braden slid the folder across his desk. Without picking it up, Ryker flipped it open and started reading. Laney had done all the online investigating. She was a whiz at hacking without leaving even the slightest clue anyone had done so. She was invaluable to the family.

Braden knew Ryker would take things over from here, which was good because Braden had no energy to put into this project right now. His mind was on Zara and the fact she'd so easily invited Ryker into her home to search.

Was she playing a game? Mocking him? Was she seriously just going to let him search with no strings attached?

As much as Braden wanted to rush over and figure out what the hell she was thinking, he also wanted to give her space. He wouldn't give her too much, but he wanted her to miss him, to realize that they were good together and his actions had been justified in the beginning.

Ryker tapped the folder on the desk. "I'll take care of it. I'm heading to my apartment, if you need me for anything."

Braden nodded and waited until Ryker had stepped out before he braced his elbows on his desk and rested his head in his palms. What the hell was he going to do? He'd messed this up. In the beginning, had he known he would've fallen for her, he would've confessed what he wanted. But he'd never known any other way than to take what he wanted and not worry about feelings or personal issues cropping up.

Braden cursed himself as he slammed his fists on to the glossy desktop. Just as he pushed away, his cell vibrated. Glancing at the screen, Braden didn't recognize the number. He wasn't in the mood to chat, but he never knew when it was a business call. For the O'Sheas, business always carried on, no matter what was going on in their private lives.

Braden grabbed the phone and slid his fingertip across the screen. "Hello."

"What the hell did you do to Zara?"

Stunned by the rage-filled tone, it took Braden a minute to place the caller. "Why are you calling me, Shane?"

"I went by her house to check on her, and she'd been crying."

Braden wasn't stupid; he figured Zara had cried, but he

wanted to give her space. Still, the thought of her alone in that big house, crying with no one to hold her, comfort her, other than the cat, gutted him.

No one, but the prick Shane.

"How the hell do you know I did anything?" Braden asked.

"Because I know you, O'Shea. And now that she's done with you, I'm moving full-force into winning her back. Just thought you should know."

That arrogant, egotistical tone slammed into him.

"You went to her house?" Braden jerked to his feet. Gripping the phone, he started for the door. "Stay away from what's mine. You won't be warned again."

Braden disconnected the call and quickly shot off a text to Ryker. Yes, he was in the same house, but Braden wasn't wasting any time. He wanted Shane dealt with right now, and while Braden would love being the one to do so himself, Braden had someone else who needed his attention even more.

Zara tugged on the old bed until it was beneath the window. She'd worked up a sweat, but finally her bedroom was rearranged. She needed it to be different, because every time she'd walked in here, she'd seen Braden. He consumed her entire home, and Zara was trying like hell to rid the house of memories. Unfortunately, they were permanently embedded into her mind, her heart.

She'd only been home an hour when her electricity kicked back on. Making good use of the time, she washed her sheets and comforter. There was no way she would've been able to crawl into bed surrounded by Braden's masculine scent… and she was almost positive Jack had an accident.

She stared over at the chaise she'd pushed near the door. She truly had no idea where to put that now that she'd changed the bed.

Zara circled her room, stopping when her eyes zeroed in

on a sock, a piece of cardboard and a small towel where her bed used to be. That kitten had started a stash.

Just the thought of the kitten, of how Braden hadn't thought twice about rescuing it, had her eyes burning all over again. She'd experienced a wide variety of emotions in the past few hours. Anger, sorrow, fury and then emptiness.

All of that stemmed from Braden. She refused to even think of all the emotions she'd felt when Shane had stopped by. Unfortunately, he'd caught her during the sorrow stage.

Zara headed down to the first floor to check on the status of her sheets. They should be dry by now, and she needed to keep focused and stay busy. She didn't want to contemplate how bored she would be once she ran out of things to do. Even work wasn't appealing to her right now.

Just as she hit the bottom step, her doorbell rang. The last thing she wanted was a visitor, especially if Shane decided to come back. Now she'd hit her anger stage, and he'd be sorry if he decided he still couldn't take no for an answer.

The stained-glass sidelights provided no clue as to who her visitor was. Zara checked the peephole in the old door and gritted her teeth. She didn't want to get into this. She truly did not want to rehash all the good, bad and sexy with the man on the other side of the door.

But she knew Braden O'Shea well enough now to know he wasn't going away without a fight. Well, if he wanted a fight, she was ready to give him one.

Jerking the door open, Zara blocked the entrance and stared at her unwelcome guest.

"Ready to search the house?" she asked sweetly.

With his hands shoved in his black wool coat, collar up around his stubbled jawline, Braden still looked sexy. Why did he have to be so damn perfect to look at?

"I don't want to search your house," he told her, his jaw clenched. "I want to talk, and if you don't want me inside, I'm more than willing to stand on your porch. The choice is yours."

She gripped the edge of the door. "I could slam this door in your face and not give you a second thought."

"You could," he agreed. "But you're not a heartless woman, Zara. And no matter what you feel now, you also still have feelings for me. You're not the type of person who can just turn those off."

Hesitating, trying to figure out what to do, Zara gave in and pushed the door wider. Turning on her socked feet, she headed into the living room. The door closed behind her, but she kept her back to the doorway because right now she couldn't even face him. If he wanted to talk, he was more than welcome to do so, but Zara didn't know if she had the strength to face him head-on.

So much for that fight she'd geared up for. Just seeing him, hearing that sultry voice thrust her back into the sorrowful stage.

"Why are you here?" she asked, wrapping her arms around her waist. "Haven't we said enough?"

"Are you going to look at me?"

Swallowing, Zara shook her head. "No."

"Fair enough."

Braden's footsteps shuffled behind her, and she braced herself for his touch, but it never came. Still, the hairs on her neck stood on end. He was close, definitely within reaching distance, yet he didn't reach for her.

"There's nothing I can say to undo what I did."

Yeah, he was so close, she could feel the warmth of his breath when he spoke. He wasn't going to make this easy on her.

"When my father was in the hospital, the doctors weren't sure if he'd make it through the heart surgery. Dad knew, though. He knew the outcome. I could tell by the way he took my hand, asked me to find these scrolls no matter what."

Zara bit her lip to keep it from trembling. Braden's words, thick with emotion, were killing her. He did all of this for

his family, the family he loved and a family that stood together through life's trials. Even though she didn't have this
type of bond, she was starting to see just how important
it was, and maybe Braden had been put in a rough place,
torn between what he wanted and what he was bound to.

"I knew I was next in line to be in charge of everything, legal or otherwise." Braden laughed. "You're the only
woman I've ever become this close to. That scares the hell
out of me, Zara. My family is… We have secrets. To know
you have that much power over me, to know that at any
moment you could turn on me and ruin my family if you
knew everything. I'm willing to risk it. That alone tells me
how much I love you."

Zara whipped around, but Braden held a finger over her
lips.

"I'm not done," he told her. "I saw how hard my dad
searched for these scrolls. We believed they were still here,
somewhere. We recovered an old trunk that had been here,
but it proved to be a dead end a couple months ago. But
when he died, I vowed to honor his wishes, to be head of
the family and someone he'd be proud of. I made it my mission to find them, no matter the cost. And I knew I had to
start with your home."

His hand slid from her lips, and she had to stop herself
from licking where he'd touched. She was still reeling from
his confession of love. Did he mean those words? Or was
he just sorry he'd actually lost at something? The scrolls…
and her.

"I knew a young woman lived here, and once I found
out your profession, I knew it would be easy to meet you.
Everything after that fell into place so fast…"

Braden shook his head, ran a hand over his face. The
stubble on his cheeks rasped against his palm. He shut his
eyes for the briefest of moments before opening them. Closing the miniscule gap between them, Braden placed his
hands on her shoulders.

"If I'd know how fast, how hard I was going to fall for you, I would've done things differently. But the past is something even I'm not powerful enough to change. All I can do is promise you I won't lie to you again."

Zara wanted to be tough, to step away from his touch, but she couldn't bring herself to move.

"What makes you think I'll believe anything you're saying?" she asked, surprised her voice came out stronger than she actually felt. "Maybe you're just upset that you didn't find the scrolls. Maybe you still need me for this house, and you want my trust back for that reason alone."

"If I wanted this house searched tomorrow, it would be done without you knowing about it."

Zara knew he was telling the truth. And yet, he hadn't sent Ryker when she'd been at Braden's house. That had to count for something…didn't it?

"Right now, all I care about is you," he went on. "I've never begged for anything in my life. I've never had to. Damn it, Zara. I have no idea what to do to get you back. I'm in territory I've never been before."

His raw honesty paralleled her own. "You think this is familiar to me?" she cried. "I've never had a man tell me he loved me. I have no idea whether or not to believe you."

Those powerful hands slid up to frame her face. Braden tipped her face up. She had no choice but to look him straight in the eye.

"You want to believe me," he murmured. "You want to believe it because your feelings are so strong and you want to hold on to that happiness… A happiness only I can give you."

Zara reached up, gripped his wrists. She wanted to pull them away, but she found herself hanging on. "I want to be done with you, Braden. I want to be over you, but I can't just ignore what I feel. You hurt me so deep. I've never been cut that deep before. My parents, guys I've dated, I've always known where I stood with them. But with you, I thought I was in one place, but I wasn't even close."

Braden's thumbs stroked her skin, sending her nerves into high gear. Why did he have to come back? Why couldn't he have just let the break be clean?

"Never again," he promised. "You'll never wonder where you stand with me. You're it for me, Zara. I know you have a fear of commitment, I know where we stand right now is shaky, but I'm not giving up. I want you in my life permanently."

One second she was listening to him profess his love, his loyalty, the next she was leaning against him, kissing him. Her mouth moved over his, her hands still gripped his wrists, but she'd needed more contact, needed Braden.

When she eased back, she licked her lips and looked into his eyes. "I can't promise you anything. All I can promise is that we work together to see where this goes. You hurt me, Braden. That's not something I can forgive so easily."

He nodded, sliding his thumb across her bottom lip. "I can understand that, and it's more than I deserve. But I'm going to be patient where you're concerned. I don't want anyone else with me. I don't want to spend my life with another woman, so if we have to take this slow for you to see how serious I am, then so be it."

She hated to bring up the bone of contention between them, but she couldn't leave it hanging in the air.

"If you want to search this house, you can."

The muscle in Braden's jaw ticked, his lids lowered and he let out a sigh. "I'm not doing anything with this house or the scrolls until you and I are on solid ground."

Zara gasped. "You're serious," she whispered.

"I've never been more serious about anyone in my life." His lips slid over hers again for a brief second. "I meant what I said about loving you. I want to fulfill my father's wishes, but I will love you first and always."

Zara threw her arms around his neck, the thick coat getting in her way when she really wanted to feel him without barriers. "I hated you," she sobbed, hating how her emotions had betrayed her, and now she was an emotional wreck. "I moved my bedroom furniture around, I washed all the blankets and sheets trying to get you out of my room."

His soft chuckle vibrated against her. "You wasted a lot of time and energy, because I'm about to take you back upstairs and make love to you."

She eased back, swiped at her face and smiled. "Everything is still in the dryer."

In a swift, unexpected move, Braden scooped her up into his arms and headed for the steps. "If I recall, our first time wasn't in the bed anyway."

Zara toyed with the ends of his hair. She didn't care where he took her, she would go. They were starting fresh, and she knew in her heart this was meant to be. He was the man who would show her what love was, show her what loyalty and commitment were.

This was the man she'd spend the rest of her life with.

Epilogue

"Calm down, Laney. What happened?"

Zara sat up, pulling the old quilt around her as she listened to the urgency in Braden's tone as he talked to his sister on the cell. The kitten snuggled against her side.

"Don't go anywhere. I'm sending Ryker. He's closer than I am."

With a curse, he disconnected the call and punched in another number.

"Is she okay?" Zara asked.

"No."

Braden reached around, tucking her against his side as he held the cell to his ear. The fact he was still seeking her during a family crisis only added to the promise he'd made only hours ago to keep her first in his life.

"Ryker." Braden's bare torso tensed as he spoke. "Go to Laney's house. She needs you to help pack some things and get her back to my house safely. Carter cheated on her, and now he's trying to get her to open her door. I just hung up with her, and she's hysterical. You're closer than I am, which means you'll need to be nice. I'll be home shortly and meet you guys there."

Once he disconnected the call, he turned into her arms. "I'm sorry."

Zara smoothed her hand over his forehead, pushing away a strand of hair. "Don't be. The fact that you're helping your sister makes me love you more."

Braden froze. "You love me?"

"I fell in love when you brought the kitten inside," she confessed. "I didn't want to admit it then or when you told me. But I can't keep it inside. I know you had your reasons for lying. I don't like them, but I understand them. I know your family loyalty runs deep, and I know when you say you love someone, you mean it."

He rested his forehead against hers. "You have no idea how relieved I am to hear you say that. To know that you believe I love you, and it has nothing to do with my family's history, this house, or those scrolls."

"Is your sister okay? Maybe we should get some clothes on and head to your place."

Braden kissed her before easing up. "Would you want to pack some things and stay with me for a while?"

Zara stared up at him, marveling at the way that body always had her complete focus. "Define a while."

He shrugged. "We can start with one day and gradually ease you into forever."

Zara smiled, jumping to her feet. "Forever. That word always scared me before."

"And now?" he asked, wrapping his arms around her and pulling her flush with his body.

She smacked his lips with her own. "And now I want to hold on to it, I want to hold on to you. Forever."

* * * * *

*If you liked TRAPPED WITH THE TYCOON,
don't miss the next MAFIA MOGULS book
from Jules Bennett:
for this tight-knit mob family,
going legitimate leads to love!*

FROM FRIEND TO FAKE FIANCÉ

Available April 2016!

And pick up Jules Bennett's

*BARRINGTON TRILOGY:
Hollywood comes to horse country—
and the Barrington family's secrets
are at the center of it all!*

*WHEN OPPOSITES ATTRACT...
SINGLE MAN MEETS SINGLE MOM
CARRYING THE LOST HEIR'S CHILD*

Only from Harlequin Desire!

***

If you're on Twitter, tell us what you think
of Harlequin Desire! #harlequindesire

#2425 His Forever Family

Billionaires and Babies • by Sarah M. Anderson

When caring for an abandoned baby brings Liberty and her billionaire boss Marcus closer, she must resist temptation. Her secrets could destroy her career and the chance to care for the foster child they are both coming to love...

#2426 The Doctor's Baby Dare

Texas Cattleman's Club: Lies and Lullabies
by Michelle Celmer

Dr. Parker Reese always gets what he wants, especially when it comes to women. When a baby shakes up his world, he decides he wants sexy nurse Clare Connelly... Will he have to risk his guarded heart to get her?

#2427 His Pregnant Princess Bride

Bayou Billionaires • by Catherine Mann

What starts as a temporary vacation fling for an arrogant heir to a Southern football fortune and a real-life princess becomes way more than they bargained for when the princess becomes pregnant!

#2428 How to Sleep with the Boss

The Kavanaghs of Silver Glen • by Janice Maynard

Ex-heiress Libby Parkhurst has nothing to lose when she takes a demanding job with Patrick Kavanagh, but her desire to impress the boss is complicated when his matchmaking family gives her a makeover that makes Patrick lose control.

#2429 Tempted by the Texan

The Good, the Bad and the Texan • by Kathie DeNosky

Wealthy rancher Jaron Lambert wants more than just one night with Mariah Stanton, but his dark past and their age difference hold him back. What will it take to push past his boundaries? Mariah's about to find out...

#2430 Needed: One Convenient Husband

The Pearl House • by Fiona Brand

To collect her inheritance, Eva Atraeus only has three weeks to marry. Billionaire banker Kyle Messena, the trustee of the will *and* her first love, rejects every potential groom...until he's the only one left! How convenient...

HDCNM0116

REQUEST YOUR FREE BOOKS!

2 FREE NOVELS PLUS 2 FREE GIFTS!

(H) HARLEQUIN®

Desire

ALWAYS POWERFUL, PASSIONATE AND PROVOCATIVE

YES! Please send me 2 FREE Harlequin® Desire novels and my 2 FREE gifts (gifts are worth about $10). After receiving them, if I don't wish to receive any more books, I can return the shipping statement marked "cancel." If I don't cancel, I will receive 6 brand-new novels every month and be billed just $4.55 per book in the U.S. or $5.24 per book in Canada. That's a savings of at least 13% off the cover price! It's quite a bargain! Shipping and handling is just 50¢ per book in the U.S. and 75¢ per book in Canada.* I understand that accepting the 2 free books and gifts places me under no obligation to buy anything. I can always return a shipment and cancel at any time. Even if I never buy another book, the two free books and gifts are mine to keep forever.

225/326 HDN GH2P

Name	(PLEASE PRINT)
Address	Apt. #
City	State/Prov.	Zip/Postal Code

Signature (if under 18, a parent or guardian must sign)

Mail to the **Reader Service**:

IN U.S.A.: P.O. Box 1867, Buffalo, NY 14240-1867
IN CANADA: P.O. Box 609, Fort Erie, Ontario L2A 5X3

Want to try two free books from another line?
Call 1-800-873-8635 or visit www.ReaderService.com.

* Terms and prices subject to change without notice. Prices do not include applicable taxes. Sales tax applicable in N.Y. Canadian residents will be charged applicable taxes. Offer not valid in Quebec. This offer is limited to one order per household. Not valid for current subscribers to Harlequin Desire books. All orders subject to credit approval. Credit or debit balances in a customer's account(s) may be offset by any other outstanding balance owed by or to the customer. Please allow 4 to 6 weeks for delivery. Offer available while quantities last.

Your Privacy—The Reader Service is committed to protecting your privacy. Our Privacy Policy is available online at www.ReaderService.com or upon request from the Reader Service.

We make a portion of our mailing list available to reputable third parties that offer products we believe may interest you. If you prefer that we not exchange your name with third parties, or if you wish to clarify or modify your communication preferences, please visit us at www.ReaderService.com/consumerchoice or write to us at Reader Service Preference Service, P.O. Box 9062, Buffalo, NY 14240-9062. Include your complete name and address.

HD15

"You have to make a decision about attending the Hanson wedding."

Marcus groaned. He did not want to watch his former fiancée get married to the man she'd cheated on him with. Unfortunately, to some, his inability to see the truth about Lillibeth until it was too late also indicated an inability to make good investment choices. So his parents had strongly suggested he attend the wedding, with an appropriate date on his arm.

All Marcus had to do was pick a woman.

"The options are limited and time is running short, Mr. Warren," Liberty said. She jammed her hands on her hips. "The wedding is in two weeks."

"Fine. I'll take you."

The effect of this statement was immediate. Liberty's eyes went wide and her mouth dropped open and her gaze dropped over his body. Something that looked a hell of a lot like desire flashed over her face.

Then it was gone. She straightened and did her best to look imperial. "Mr. Warren, be serious."

"I am serious. I trust you." He took a step toward her. "Sometimes I think…you're the only person who's honest with me. I want to take you to the wedding."

It was hard to say if she blushed, as she was already red-faced from their morning run and the heat. But something in her expression changed. "No," she said flatly. Before he could take the rejection personally, she added, "I—it—would be bad for you."

He could hear the pain in her voice. He took another step toward her and put a hand on her shoulder. She looked up, her eyes wide and—hopeful? His hand drifted from her shoulder to her cheek and damned if she didn't lean into his touch. "How could you be bad for me?"

The moment the words left his mouth, he realized he'd pushed this too far.

She shut down. She stepped away and turned to face the lake. "We need to head back to the office."

That's when he heard a noise. Marcus looked around, trying to find the source. A shoe box on the ground next to a trash can moved.

Marcus's stomach fell in. Oh, no—who would throw away a kitten? He hurried over to the box and pulled the lid off and—

Sweet Jesus. Not a kitten.

A baby.

Don't miss
HIS FOREVER FAMILY by Sarah M. Anderson
available February 2016 wherever
Harlequin® Desire books and ebooks are sold.

www.Harlequin.com

Love the Harlequin book you just read?

Your opinion matters.

Review this book on your favorite book site, review site, blog or your own social media properties and share your opinion with other readers!

HARLEQUIN®

A *Romance* FOR EVERY MOOD™

JUST CAN'T GET ENOUGH?

Join our social communities
and talk to us online.

You will have access to the latest
news on upcoming titles and special
promotions, but most importantly,
you can talk to other fans about your
favorite Harlequin reads.

Harlequin.com/Community

 Facebook.com/HarlequinBooks

 Twitter.com/HarlequinBooks

 Pinterest.com/HarlequinBooks